God's Will

The Mystery Now Made Known

William Childers

Copyright © 2003 by William Childers

God's Will
by William Childers

Printed in the United States of America

Library of Congress Control Number: 2002117080
ISBN 1-591604-16-8

All rights reserved. No part of this publication may be reproduced or transmitted in any form or by any means without written permission of the publisher.

Unless otherwise stated, Bible quotations are taken from King James Version of the Bible, Thomas Nelson Inc. Publishers, Copyright © 1975 and The Holy Bible, New International Version, New York International Bible Society, Copyright © 1978.

Words appearing in brackets within quoted Scriptures are inserted by the author.

Xulon Press
11350 Random Hills Road
Suite 800
Fairfax, VA 22030
(703) 279-6511
XulonPress.com

To order additional copies, call 1-866-909-BOOK (2665).

CONTENTS

1. THE WILL..11
   THE WILL OF GOD—.............................13
   THE MYSTERY NOW MADE KNOWN........15

2. THE OLD WILL OF GOD.........................21
   THE PROMISE OF A NEW COVENANT......25

3. TERMS OF A WILL.................................31

4. THE NEW WILL OF GOD........................67
   THE WILL OF GOD PREAMBLE................68

5. THE WILL OF GOD PART ONE................83

6. THE WILL OF GOD PART TWO..............105

7. THE WILL OF GOD PART THREE..........113

8. THE WILL OF GOD PART FOUR...........153

Bibliography...175

A TEACHER'S PRAYER

Father God, my mind's ability to understand and reason, in comparison to Yours, is like a grain of sand on a million miles of beach.

Help my human mind to be a worthy receiver of Your Word, and then teach others, but always remind me of this comparison.

—*William D. Childers*

Preface

Why study the Will of God? Jesus said,

> "Not everyone that saith unto me, Lord, Lord, shall enter the kingdom of heaven; but he that doeth *the will of my Father* which is in heaven. Many will say to me in that day, Lord, Lord, have we not prophesied in thy name? and in thy name have cast out devils? and in thy name done many wonderful works? And then will I profess unto them, I never knew you: depart from me, ye that work iniquity."
>
> Matthew 7:21-23

> "Wherefore he saith, Awake thou that sleepest, and arise from the dead, and Christ shall give thee light. See then that ye walk circumspectly [cautiously], not as fools, but as wise, Redeeming [making good] the time, because the days are evil. Wherefore be ye not unwise, but understanding what the w*ill of the Lord* is."
>
> Ephesians 5:14-17

CHAPTER 1

THE WILL

If someone would come to you with the news that the richest man on earth, having untold wealth, had made you heir to all that he possessed, i.e., land, stocks, bonds, cattle, real estate, motels, hotels, resorts, automobiles, and condominiums in Hawaii, Italy, Spain, Sweden, London, Tokyo, Hong Kong, and the United States of America, with cash in banks around the world, you, chances are, would become overjoyed to say the least.

Then you would probably doubt that such a *will* exists. So you begin to check on the validity of such a *will*, and find it to be real.

You further find that the testator had died, making this *will* valid and ready to be received by you. Now you're ecstatic! You say to yourself, *Whom should I see about this? What must I do to prove that I am the heir?*

You now proceed to produce a birth certificate, family history, Social Security I.D., history of employment, past IRS records, place of birth, locations of all places you have lived, everything else you can "dig up" to prove you are the true heir to this vast sum of wealth.

Your first step is to find the person who told you about

the *will*, apologize for not believing him, then ask him who you should see to claim your inheritance. After you locate the individual, he directs you to the person who is the mediator of the *will*.

By this time you're walking three feet off the ground, almost ready to explode with excitement. As you come face to face with the mediator, your hands are shaking like a "leaf in a windstorm." The briefcase in your hand is rattling with all the evidence of who you are.

The mediator speaks, and you almost stop breathing. "Welcome! Why has it taken so long for you to come to me? I know all about you, and where you come from. You don't need the evidence in your briefcase. All that is needed on your part is to accept the fact that you are the heir, and receive it."

Can you imagine how you would rejoice if this person was you?

There is good news today! God, your Heavenly Father, has written His *Will*, and you can be an heir. Jesus Christ, the Son of God, mediator of the *Will*, and the one who died to validate the Will, rose from the grave, and is now sitting at the right hand of the Father offering God's *Will* to you. Jesus brought the Word (*Will*) to mankind.

This book is a description of *God's Will*. Read on and see if you want to receive all that God the Father has for you.

THE WILL OF GOD

TO ALL who repent of their sins and believe that I am the only true and living God, I, God the Father, God the Son, and God the Holy Spirit, do will the following:

Part One. I want you to have the finest things that life has to offer. Please accept the guide to a happy, prosperous, healthy, and successful life found in Exodus 20:1-17. These words were written that you might have a better understanding of perfect love for both Me and your neighbor. Know them, for they can keep you from heartbreak and bitter tears in the late hours at night. My love for you is beyond your fullest understanding. Keep these words in your heart that you might know happiness as an individual, a nation, or as a universe.

Part Two. Since the dawn of creation I have watched you make mistakes, and I have watched you cry bitterly because of the results of sin. So dear friend, I sent My Son, Jesus, to shed His blood that you could better know how I feel for you. Jesus dwelt among you in the form of flesh like yourself. He was tempted just like you are tempted. Therefore, He knows how to help you and judge mankind. He died that you need never sacrifice an animal for the forgiveness of sin. Now He sits here beside Me and tells Me your cares both good and bad. He also tells Me about the things you are thankful for. My Son, Jesus, will hear your prayers if you are sincere. Jesus is part of My Will for you—that you might have life more abundantly. Please accept Him as your friend.

God's Will

You could not possibly have a better friend, for it is through Him we shall meet someday.

Part Three. I can see your weakness and inability to cope with sin and the problems of your world. Through Jesus I sent the Holy Spirit into this world of yours that you might have strength to overcome sin and the wisdom you need to understand the things of this Will. I will to you the gift of the Holy Spirit. There are nine gifts of the Spirit which you may seek. They are part of My Will for you, but of all the gifts I promised, place love at the top. Love for your Creator and love for your neighbor.

Part Four. The fourth part of My Will to you is eternal life with Us. Yes, life without end. Please believe Me when I say it is *not* My Will that any should perish. I am preparing a place for you that will be beyond your grandest imagination. Life eternal is My Will for you. At times it may seem that I am not close to you, but I am.

Dear friend, this is My Will for you. All you need to do is to accept it.

© W.D. Childers 1974 A.D.

THE WILL OF GOD THE MYSTERY NOW MADE KNOWN

What is *God's Will* for me? Can I know *the Will of God*? Is *God's Will* something that will always be secret? Can you please tell me what *God's Will* is? These are questions you may have pondered.

We need to explain briefly what a will is. Then as we travel through this book you will see the fog clear away, and the *Will of God* shall no longer be a mystery. If this *Will of God* is new to you, just keep reading and let it thrill you because this present mystery is not fiction, but fact and it is for you.

> "He [Jesus] answered and said unto them, Because it is given unto you to know the mysteries of the kingdom of heaven . . . "
> Matthew 13:11

There are several definitions for the word *will*. The definition we will use is concerning a legal document. A last *will* and *testament* is a document in which the testator is leaving to his heirs something of great value. The value may be a title, position, land, wealth, etc.[1]

God has made for you a valid *Will*. Jesus Christ of Nazareth wrote the Testament *(Will)* which we call the *New Testament*. He also wrote the Old Testament, which was given to Abram and his descendants. The *Will of God* is not a myth. It is as real as the earth we stand on. Jesus is the Son of God, and also God the Son, with full authority to present both *Wills*.

Stop here and turn in your Bible to Hebrews 9:15-17.

God's Will

"And for this cause he [Jesus] is the mediator of the *new testament*, that by means of death, for the redemption of the transgressions that were under the *first testament,* they which are called, might receive the promise of eternal inheritance."
Hebrews 9:15

I will explain this in greater detail in chapter 3. Key points for your consideration now are:

(1) Jesus was the mediator for conveying this gift from the Father God to mankind.

(2) The Will was only by faith and on paper until by Jesus' death, it became valid.

(3) There is an eternal inheritance. You inherit something through a will or testament.

Jesus came *to do God's Will*. Everything that was done by Jesus was in unity with the Father God. Both the Old and New *Wills* were planned by the Father, Jesus, and the Holy Spirit. The creation was carried out by Jesus, but came from the Father. The Ten Commandments were written by Jesus, but came from the Father. Jesus brought the *Will of God*, old and new, put it in writing, and gave it to man.

"For where a testament is, there must also of necessity be the death of the testator [the one making the will]. For a testament [or will] is of force after men are dead: otherwise it is of no strength at all while the testator liveth."
Hebrews 9:16,17

Key thoughts in verses 16 and 17 are:

The Will

(1) The testator must die in order that the one to receive the benefits of a will can in fact do so.

(2) A will has no strength until the testator dies. The Creator had to die, by law, in order for all mankind to receive His Will.

So now you can clearly see I am talking about a *Will*, or Testament from God.
There are actually two *Wills*. The *Old Testament* (or *Will*), and the *New Testament*. Have you wondered why the Bible is divided and named The *Old Testament* and The *New Testament*? It is because there are two different Wills. *The Will of God* shall be received by those who are willing to accept it, to those willing to do as He, Jesus, directs.

"Not every one that saith unto me, Lord, Lord, shall enter into the kingdom of heaven; but he that doeth the will of my Father which is in heaven."
Matthew 7:21

The *Old Will of God* was given to Abram (Abraham) and his descendants, because of Abram's faith in God. The Lord appeared to Abram and said,

" . . . walk before me, and be thou perfect."
Genesis 17:1

Abram's love for God and man was perfect. He kept the commands of God. He did what God wanted him to do. He was willing to give his son Isaac as a sacrifice to God, because God asked him to do so. God was only testing his willingness to obey, but Abram held true to God. Abram's descendants were to do as God commanded, and they would receive Canaan as an inheritance. Canaan, as you may know,

God's Will

is called Israel.

When I talk about commandments here, I am not talking about the Ten Commandments that were given four hundred and thirty years later (Galatians 3:17). I am talking about verbal commandments God gave to Abraham for his descendants. The Ten Commandments were given because of Israel's transgressions (sins) (Galatians 3:19).

When Jesus died on the cross, He redeemed (made good His promise) to the Old Testament saints. He died to make valid the *Old Will of God*, so that on the Resurrection Day, all Abram's descendants who did the *Old Will* as instructed will rise from their graves and live again in Canaan, and on into everlasting life.

Since the dawn of creation man has struggled with sin. All through the *Old Testament* you can read how the children of Israel, God's chosen people, would have great and prosperous days, then sin would take over again, bringing them down like a punctured balloon. Their history of success and failure is repeated over and over.

God, seeing man's inability to cope with sin, sent Jesus His Son into this world to bring new hope through the *New Will*.

Jesus lived as man among men and learned how sin can change man into the evil one's slave. The devil can disguise sin to look and feel as though it's the most wonderful thing in this world. Then sin and all its terror will come crashing down on man like a wall of horror.

Sin appears at first to be like a beautiful gold link in a chain, each sin adding another bright shining link. Then the chain becomes heavier and longer, wrapping and binding you until your body cries out in pain. The chains of sin break the body, soul, and spirit, making a person much less than he or she could be, and often, a physical or mental wreck.

The *New Will of God* brought hope for all. Jesus became the last blood sacrifice for sin and the mediator of the *New*

The Will

Will. Now Jesus sits at the right hand of God the Father in heaven, and tells Him in words that neither you nor I could ever utter, just how tough sin can be on the human spirit. When you pray, He is ready and willing to do for you exceedingly and abundantly above all that you can ask or think if you accept and do the *Will of God*. Could you have a better friend?

The Ten Commandments were given to us as a guide to what love really is, but man has failed to understand this. Because of this inability to understand, God gave us the Holy Spirit to be with us all the time. This gift was given from the Father God, through Jesus Christ, so that we may have strength, wisdom, faith, and understanding to accept and do the *Will*, and to understand His love as written in the Ten Commandments.

God the Father, through Jesus Christ, has also offered us eternal life through His *Will*. Living with God the Father, God the Son, and God the Holy Spirit eternally, is beyond our greatest imagination. We cannot comprehend living in a city where streets are pure gold, fifteen hundred miles square and fifteen hundred miles high (Revelation 21:16). There will be no more sorrow, sickness, pain, or hunger. The benefits of doing the *Will of God* certainly outweigh the pleasures of sin.

My hope is that you too will examine the total *Will of God* and accept it by faith, as did Abraham, then begin to experience the peace of mind and love of God that I have attempted to explain. It is all for you. God planned that no one should perish, but He certainly is not going to rope, tie, and brand you a Christian if you don't want it. God is love, and love gives man a choice.

I hope you will probe the Scriptures referenced in this book. I pray that the Holy Spirit will help you to completely understand the Scriptures concerning the total *Will of God*.

Chapter 1

Summary

God planned a will for you and me, a will that was once a mystery. His Will came first to Abraham and his descendants, but now a New Will has been given to all people. Every nation, tribe, man, woman, boy, girl, bond, or free is eligible to receive this wonderful Will, one that is already valid and ready for you to receive by faith.

Jesus, the Son of God, brought both the Old and New Wills to mankind from Father God. Jesus was also the testator of both wills and by His death both Wills became valid and are now ready for you and me to receive.

CHAPTER 2

THE OLD WILL OF GOD

I would venture to say there are a lot of people who do not know what the *Old Will of God* was. So, in order to understand the *New Will of God* better, we should understand the Old Will and why it was replaced.

God noticed Abram's faith, so God gave a promise to him. God told Abram to walk perfectly before Him and He would bless him. God changed Abram's name to Abraham, then told him he would be the father of many nations.

In Genesis 22, God tested Abraham's willingness to obey. His willingness to sacrifice his only son to God was to be rewarded. Abraham was ready and willing to obey the voice of God. He not only was willing, but also did obey. There is a big difference.

> The *Old Will of God*—What was it, and to whom was it given?
> The *Old Will of God* is all the land of Canaan.

"And I will give unto thee, and to thy seed after thee, the land wherein thou art a stranger, all the land of Canaan, for an everlasting possession; and

I will be their God."

Genesis 17:8

Canaan is the land God swore to give to Abraham, Isaac, and Jacob (Genesis 50:24).

Abraham received the *Will* from God. Isaac was the only son of Abraham. Isaac had two sons, Jacob and Esau. God rejected Esau because of his disobedience. Jacob's name was changed to Israel. God said to him in Genesis 35:10: "Thy name shall not be called anymore Jacob, but Israel." Jacob had twelve sons who became known as the children of Israel.

This is the Will of God given to Abraham and his descendants.

> "Therefore say, Thus saith the Lord God; I will even gather you from the people, and assemble you out of the countries where ye have been scattered, and I will give you the land of Israel [which is the land of Canaan]."
>
> Ezekiel 11:17

COVENANT

God gave a covenant to Abram. *Covenant* has basically the same meaning as a *will* or *testament*.

Covenant is defined as the solemn promises of God to man as set forth in the *Old* and *New Testaments*; compact between God and man; He hath remembered His covenant forever.[1]

The *covenant* was first made with Abram in Genesis 12:1-7, and again in Genesis 15:18-21. Read the entire chapter, for in it God enters into a blood covenant with Abram in answer to Abram's request (Genesis 15:8): "Whereby shall

I know that I shall inherit it?" Verses 9-21 describe how this blood *covenant* was performed. Read this for yourself. Praise God, there is no need for such sacrifices today.

Jesus was the paschal lamb of sacrifice, the last such sacrifice, for by His death, and by His last *Will* and *Testament*, we can all inherit eternal life.

It is interesting to read the boundaries of this Promised Land. Genesis 15:18: "From the river of Egypt unto the great river, the river Euphrates." This Promised Land (covenant) is much larger than I once thought.

> "O ye seed of Abraham his servant, ye children of Jacob his chosen. He is the Lord our God: his judgments are in all the earth. He hath remembered his covenant forever, the word which he commanded to a thousand generations. Which covenant he made with Abraham, and his oath unto Isaac; And confirmed the same unto Jacob for a law, and to Israel for an everlasting covenant: Saying, Unto thee will I give the land of Canaan, the lot of your inheritance."
> Psalm 105:6-11

Genesis 17 tells again about the *covenant* and the sign or token of the *covenant* between God and Abraham as well as all Abraham's descendants.

> "And ye shall circumcise the flesh of your foreskin; and it shall be a token of the covenant betwixt me and you."
> Genesis 17:11

The Hebrew blood *covenant* is circumcision. Circumcision for the Jew is the sign of the "berith," the *covenant* between God and Israel established first with

God's Will

Abraham, then later at Sinai, to be passed on through every generation until the end of time.

> "And the Lord spoke unto Moses, saying, Speak unto the children of Israel, saying, If a woman have conceived seed, and born a man child . . . And in the eighth day the flesh of his foreskin shall be circumcised."
>
> Leviticus 12:1-3

One day the promised covenant will be realized:

> "Thus saith the Lord God; Behold, O my people, I will open your graves, and cause you to come up out of your graves, and bring you into the land of Israel . . . And shall put my spirit in you, and ye shall live, and I shall place you in your own land: then shall ye know that I the Lord have spoken it, and performed it, saith the Lord."
>
> Ezekiel 37:12,14

As I see it, all the saints of the house of Israel will be resurrected, and shall one day be living in their Promised Land.

> "And David my servant shall be king over them; and they all shall have one shepherd: they shall also walk in my judgments, and observe my statutes, and do them."
>
> Ezekiel 37:24

Now read Ezekiel 36. Here Ezekiel is telling about the future restoration of Israel. Verse 12 talks about an inheritance. You inherit something through a *will*. Then in verse 24 He (God) says that the Israelites will be taken out from the heathen, and brought into their land. As yet, this has only partially happened. Next, verse 26 states, "A new heart also will I give you, and a new spirit . . . " This also has not yet happened. I feel it will happen at the Resurrection. Verse 28 tells us, "Ye shall dwell in the land that I gave to your fathers." In verse 30 He (God) will multiply the fruit of the tree and increase the field. Verse 33 says, "In the day that I shall have cleansed you from all your iniquities I will also cause you to dwell in the cities." Then verse 35 states that the land will become as the Garden of Eden.

"And I will bring forth a seed out of Jacob, and out of Judah an inheritor of my mountains: and mine elect shall inherit it, and my servants shall dwell there."

Isaiah 65:9

THE PROMISE OF A NEW COVENANT

Read Jeremiah 31:31-34. Here Jeremiah talks about a new *covenant*. I first thought that this New *Will of God*, or *covenant*, was referring to the Holy Ghost dispensation, but after more careful study I feel that the new covenant is referring to the new kingdom of Israel. Verse 31 tells of a new covenant with the house of Israel and with Judah. In verse 32 the *Will* is not like the one made to the Israelites in Egypt, because they did not keep the covenant. They broke God's commandments. In verse 33 He (the Lord) states that in this New Will the law will be written in their inward parts and they will be God's people. Verse 34 states that they will no longer teach their neighbor to know the Lord. They will know the Lord from the least to the greatest. God told them that He would remember their sins no more. Also read about the new covenant in Hebrews 8:6-13. Doesn't that sound like everlasting life for the Old Testament saints? What a

God's Will

wonderful resurrection that will be!

Does this mean that all the house of Israel will be raised from the dead and live forevermore? In light of what David said in Psalm 1, I would say no.

> "Therefore the ungodly shall not stand in the judgment, nor sinners in the congregation of the righteous. For the Lord knoweth the way of the righteous: but the way of the ungodly shall perish."
> Psalm 1:5,6

Not all of Abraham's descendants will be resurrected to Canaan.

> "He that keepeth the commandment keepeth his own soul; but he that despiseth his ways [God's ways] shall die."
> Proverbs 19:16

When the Israelites escaped from Egypt, the sin of unbelief kept them from entering into Canaan and I think the unrighteous will not be resurrected to Canaan (Israel). When the final judgment begins, which I feel will come after the thousand-year reign of Jesus Christ here on earth, those who kept not His *Will*, shall only hear these terrible words:

> "And then will I profess unto them, I never knew you: depart from me, ye that work iniquity."
> Matthew 7:23

They, like those who still refuse to believe and do the *Will of God* will be cast into the lake of fire, which is the second death and eternal punishment for all who want to hurt or destroy that which is good.

The Old Will of God

"And whosoever was not found written in the book of life was cast into the lake of fire."
Revelation 20:15

"He that overcometh shall inherit all things; and I will be his God, and he shall be my son. But the fearful, and unbelieving, and the abominable, and murderers, and whoremongers, and sorcerers, and idolaters, and all liars, shall have their part in the lake which burneth with fire and brimstone: which is the second death."
Revelation 21:7,8

Brimstone is sulfur. It burns with a blue flame (very hot) has a very stifling odor (it smells like rotten eggs). This is not a very friendly atmosphere to be placed into. If you go there, I don't think you will notice your friends there.

God asks that He should have first place in your life, because He is love. If we have God, who is love, and have Him at the center of our lives, we will have love for our neighbor. True love. When we allow God to have first place in our lives, we then have the first part of the *Will of God*. We have love. When we completely understand this, we then understand the first three of the Ten Commandments and part of the fourth. We will discuss this further in Part One, *The Will of God*.

Read what the Book of Daniel has to say about Canaan. Daniel 2:44 says God shall set up a kingdom to stand forever. Daniel 4:17 says, "The most high ruleth in the kingdom of men, and giveth it to whomsoever He will." Verse 32 repeats, "Giveth it to whomsoever he will." Verse 35 says, "He doeth according to his will in the army of heaven, and among the inhabitants of the earth." Daniel 5:21 says, "God ruled in the kingdom of men, and that he appointeth over it whomsoever he will." Daniel 7:14 tells us His kingdom shall

God's Will

not be destroyed. Verse 18 says, "The saints of the most High shall take the kingdom, and possess the kingdom forever, even forever and ever." Verse 22 declares, "The saints possessed the kingdom."

> "And the kingdom and dominion [supreme authority], and the greatness of the kingdom under the whole heaven, shall be given to the people of the saints of the most High, whose kingdom is an everlasting kingdom, and all dominions shall serve and obey him."
>
> Daniel 7:27

> "And I prayed unto the Lord my God, and made my confession, and said, O Lord, the great and dreadful God, keeping the *covenant* and mercy to them that love him, and to them that keep his commandments."
>
> Daniel 9:4

Can you imagine the tremendous joy the children of Israel must have felt, knowing they belong to the family of Abraham? Remember this, there was no hope of everlasting life for those outside this family. Jesus brought to mankind a new *Will*, one that includes all who are willing to obey Him. By this *Will* we are heirs because we can all become sons and daughters of God, by the *New Will and Testament of God*.

Chapter 2

Summary

Abraham received God's first Will by faith. It was called a covenant. A blood covenant was made with Abraham because he questioned whether or not he would receive the promised inheritance. Abraham and all his descendants are to be circumcised as a token sign of the blood covenant between God and Abraham.

A promise of a new covenant was given from God to Jeremiah concerning Israel and Judah. In this new covenant, the law will be written in their inward parts. They will know the Lord. They will no longer need to teach their neighbor to know the Lord.

The Old Will of God was and is all the land of Canaan, given to Abraham, Isaac, and Jacob. Jacob's name was changed to Israel.

CHAPTER 3

TERMS OF A WILL

Chapter 3 is a study of words relating to a *will* or *testament*. We will examine the words *testament, testator, heir, inherit, inheritance, ransom, will,* and *redeem,* providing ample Scriptures to make firm we are talking about a *will* from God.

We now know about the *Old Will of God*, but where does that leave us, we who may or may not be descendants of Abraham.

Now would be a good time to define the word *testament* in light of what you have read up to now, and begin to bring into focus the new *Will of God*, written for all mankind, i.e., for those who will accept and do His *Will*.

TESTAMENT

Testament: Written instructions telling what to do with a person's property after his death; Covenant with God, Holy Scripture, last will, to be a witness, call to witness, make a will.[2]

Hebrews 7:22 tells us we have a better *testament* through Jesus Christ. Verse 24 says Jesus is the continual, unchangeable priesthood. Verse 25 assures us God is able to save to the uttermost those who will come to God by Him. He lives to make intercession for us to God the Father. Verse 26 says He is the high priest who is holy, harmless, undefiled, separate from sinners and made higher than the heavens. Verse 27 tells us He does not need to make a sacrifice for sins daily. He offered himself for a sacrifice once for *all* who will accept Him. Hebrews 10:10 says, "By the which will we are sanctified through the offering of the body of Jesus Christ once for *all*."

Jesus is the mediator of a better *covenant (will)*.

> "But now hath he obtained a more excellent ministry, by how much also he is the mediator of a better covenant, which was established upon better promises. For if that first covenant had been faultless, then should no place have been sought for the second."
>
> Hebrews 8:6,7

Hebrews 9:1-10 tells us the first *covenant* had divine services. The writer of Hebrews describes the tabernacle and what was in it, and how the priests accomplished the service of God. He describes the duties of the high priest and how he offered a blood sacrifice for himself and for the errors of the people.

> "But Christ being come an high priest of good things to come, by a greater and more perfect tabernacle, not made with hands, that is to say, not of this building."
>
> Hebrews 9:11

Terms of a Will

Jesus was God the Father's lamb of sacrifice and the eternal redemption (salvation) for us *all*, both Jew and Gentile.

> "How much more shall the blood of Christ, who through the eternal Spirit offered himself without spot to God, purge your conscience from dead works to serve the living God? And for this cause he is the mediator of the *new testament*, that by means of death, for the redemption of the transgressions that were under the first *testament*, they which are called might receive the promise of eternal inheritance. For where a *testament [will]* is, there must also of necessity be the death of the testator. For a *testament* is of force after men are dead: otherwise it is of no strength at all while the testator liveth."
> Hebrews 9:14-17

The blood of bulls and goats cannot take sins away (Hebrews 10:4).

> "Wherefore when he cometh into the world, he saith, Sacrifice and offering thou wouldest not, but a body hast thou prepared me: In burnt offerings and sacrifices for sin thou hast had no pleasure. Then said I, Lo, I come (in the volume of the book it is written of me) to do thy will, O God."
> Hebrews 10:5-7

The *New Will of God* is now the only hope of eternal life. This *New Will* now supersedes the *Old Will*, but not for those who died under the *Old Will*. The *Old Testament* saints will be resurrected, by faith, through the *Old Testament* (*Will*) because of Jesus' death on the cross.

God's Will

TESTATOR

Testator: A person who makes a will; A person who died leaving a valid will.[1]

"For where a testament is, there must also of necessity be the death of the testator. For a testament is of force after men are dead: otherwise it is of no strength at all while the testator liveth."
                                                    Hebrews 9:16,17

After the death of a person who has written a will, the heir can possess that which was willed to him.

Moses shed the blood of animals for the sins of the people, "Saying, This is the blood of the *testament* which God hath enjoined unto you . . . Without shedding of blood is no remission of sins" (Hebrews 9:20,22).

Now at the end time, Jesus has appeared to put away sacrifice of animals and gave himself, and to those who look for Him, He shall appear again the second time unto salvation. Christ was offered once for the sins of many. Look for Him to come again without sin unto salvation. It is impossible for the blood of bulls and goats to take away sins. The *Old Testament* blood sacrifices were symbols of that which was to come. Jesus Christ was the *testator* of the *Old Will* of God, and by His death (blood sacrifice) the *Old Will* became valid (Hebrews 9:19-28 and Hebrews 10:4).

We will look at a few verses in Hebrews 10, but it would be good to read this entire chapter for yourself. Jesus Christ came into the world to do the *Will of God*. He came to finish the first *Will* and to establish the second or last *Will*. Through this last *Will* we are sanctified, through the offering of His body. Now Jesus is sitting at the right hand of the Father, until His enemies become His footstool. If we sin willfully now that the last sacrifice was made for sin, there

Terms of a Will

remains no more sacrifice. His adversaries shall be devoured. In other words, an animal sacrifice is no longer acceptable in the sight of God, nor will there be anymore sacrifice on God's part. In the end, all His enemies, those who are evil in the sight of God, those who do not do God's *Will*, shall perish.

How much greater do you suppose God's wrath to be, when you deliberately trod God's Son under your feet by sinning, insulting the Spirit of Grace? If we do the *Will of God*, we shall receive the promise. The just shall live by faith. But we are not of them who draw back into destruction, but of them who believe to the saving of the soul (Hebrews 10).

In Matthew 26 Jesus is speaking to His disciples at the Last Supper (Lord's Supper). Raising His cup He spoke these words:

> "Drink ye all of it; For this is my blood [a symbol of His blood] of the *New Testament*, which is shed for many for the remission [forgiveness] of sins."
> Matthew 26:28

The shed blood and death of Jesus were necessary to make valid the *Old Will* as well as the *New Will*. Here, Jesus is making it known that He must die, for it was He who wrote both *Wills*. They really did not understand that which He spoke, and even now, many do not understand. Jesus brought the *Wills* from the Father God. He did only as the Father told Him. There has never been, nor shall there ever be, a greater sacrifice made than was made for you and me. Jesus was the *testator.*

Both Mark and Luke record this Last Supper statement by Jesus. Mark 14:24 records: "This is my blood of the *new testament.*" Luke 22:20 tells us: "This cup is the *new testament* in my blood, which is shed for you." Jesus was speak-

God's Will

ing symbolically of His own blood that would be shed on the cross bringing about His death, and our eternal blessings through His wonderful *Will.*

John does not mention the word *testament,* but uses the word *will* in its place. Look at John 1:10-13: "The world was made by him, and the world knew him not. He came unto his own [the children of Israel], and his own received him not. But as many as received him, to them gave he power to become the sons of God, even to them that believe on his name: Which were born, not of blood, nor of the will of the flesh, nor of the will of man, but of God." Yes, born again by the *Will of God.*

> "And Jesus said unto them, I am the bread of life: he that cometh to me shall never hunger; and he that believeth on me shall never thirst . . . For I came down from heaven, not to do mine own *will,* but the *will* of him [Father God] that sent me. And this is the Father's *will* which hath sent me, that of all which he hath given me I should lose nothing, but should raise it up again at the last day. And this is the *will* of him that sent me, that every one which seeth the Son, and believeth on him, may have everlasting life: and I will raise him up at the last day."
>
> John 6:35,38-40

This is a very definite promise for those who believe.

In the following Scripture, Jesus is speaking of spiritual things, and is hard to understand. In John 6:40-58, Jesus said that unless you believe that He is the Bread of Life (eternal life) and believe that by His shed blood (or by His death) you can inherit eternal life, you will not receive eternal life. In fact, unless you believe you cannot receive the *Will* of the Father God. If you do as Jesus has asked, He will raise you up on the last day.

> "This is that bread which came down from heaven: not as your fathers did eat manna, and are dead: he that eateth of this bread shall live forever."
>
> John 6:58

I shall praise God forever! Jesus is that Bread of Life.

> "Take heed therefore unto yourselves, and to all the flock, over the which the Holy Ghost hath made you overseers, to feed the church of God, which he hath purchased with his own blood."
>
> Acts 20:28

Being justified by His blood (death), we shall be saved from wrath through Him. He is the *testator* (Romans 5:9).

> "The cup of blessing which we bless, is it not the communion of the blood of Christ? The bread which we break, is it not the communion of the body of Christ? For we being many are one bread, and one body: for we are all partakers of that one bread."
>
> 1 Corinthians 10:16,17

> "And when he had given thanks, he brake it, and said, Take, eat: this is my body, which is broken for you: this do in remembrance of me. After the same manner also he took the cup, when he had supped, saying, This cup is the new *testament* in my blood: this do ye, as oft as ye drink it, in remembrance of me."
>
> 1 Corinthians 11:24,25

"Giving thanks unto the Father, which hath made us meet [fit] to be partakers of the inheritance of the saints in light: Who hath delivered us from the power of darkness, and hath translated us into the kingdom of his dear Son: In whom we have redemption through his blood, even the forgiveness of sins."
Colossians 1:12-14

"Forasmuch then as the children are partakers of flesh and blood, he also himself likewise took part of the same; that through death he might destroy him that had the power of death, that is, the devil."
Hebrews 2:14

"Neither by the blood of goats and calves, but by his own blood he entered in once into the holy place, having obtained eternal redemption for us."
Hebrews 9:12

I have mentioned only a few places in the Scriptures relating to the blood (or death) of the *testator*, Jesus Christ. You may want to look up more verses on the blood, and that would be a fine thing to do.

"Now the God of peace, that brought again from the dead our Lord Jesus, that great shepherd of the sheep, through the blood of the everlasting *covenant*, Make you perfect in every good work to do his *will*, working in you that which is well-pleasing in his sight, through Jesus Christ; to whom be glory for ever and ever. Amen."
Hebrews 13:20,21

Terms of a Will

HEIR

An heir is the person receiving the benefits of a will. An heir receives or has the right to receive someone's property or title after the death of its owner.[1] Haven't you always wanted to be an *heir* to some great and wonderful possession? Good news for you, friend! You can be *heir* and joint *heir* with Jesus, God's only Son. Can this really be true? Yes, it is really true.

Matthew 21:33-46 speaks of an *heir* and his inheritance. Here, Jesus is referring to himself and the *Will of God*. Search out this truth for yourself. The chief priests and Pharisees understood who Jesus was talking about and they wanted to kill Him, but they feared the crowds. In verse 43 we can see that not everyone will inherit the kingdom of God. Be careful that you don't lose your inheritance. Accept Jesus, do His *Will*, and be an *heir.*

Romans 8:14 says, "For as many as are led by the Spirit of God, they are sons of God." If we are children of God, then we are *heirs* of God, and joint *heirs* with Jesus Christ (verse 17). We then shall inherit the kingdom of God and receive the title of sons of God, because Jesus is the Son of God.

Galatians 3:26 says we are all the children of God by faith in Christ Jesus. Verse 28 explains that it makes no difference if you are Jew or Greek, bond or free, male or female: we are all one in Christ Jesus. Verse 29 says, "And if ye be Christ's, then are ye Abraham's seed, and *heirs* according to the promise." How about that! We are now Abraham's seed. Praise the Lord!

Belonging to the family of Abraham is a very significant point. We who were outside the family of Abraham had no hope of eternal life until Jesus included *all* who are in Christ Jesus. This brings *all* of us into the *Will of God*, i.e., all who will accept and do the *Will of God*.

God's Will

"Not every one that saith unto me, Lord, Lord, shall enter into the kingdom of heaven; but he that doeth the will of my Father which is in heaven. Many will say to me in that day, Lord, Lord, have we not prophesied in thy name? and in thy name have cast out devils? and in thy name done many wonderful works? And then will I profess unto them, I never knew you: depart from me, ye that work iniquity [evil wicked ways]."
Matthew 7:21-23

Galatians 4:7 tells us we are no longer a servant but a son; and if a son, then an *heir* of God through Jesus Christ, if we believe and receive this wonderful *Will of God*. No more a servant, but a son. Are you a son of God? You can be through His wonderful *Will*.

Ephesians 3:6 says the Gentiles should be fellow *heirs—should*, i.e., we can be, if we choose to receive His *Will*, and do it.

"That being justified by his grace, we should be made heirs according to the hope of eternal life."
Titus 3:7

Hebrews 1:2 explains that Jesus is *heir* of all things. Just think of it! We are joint heirs with Jesus. Fantastic! Can it get any better? I don't think so!

Hebrews 11:7 tells us Noah became *heir* to righteousness by faith. This is interesting since the Old Testament (*Will*), had not yet been given. As far as I can find the Ten Commandments had not yet been written. Noah did according to the direct verbal commandments, and became *heir* by faith. I can't help but feel that the Ten Commandments may have been passed down from Adam and Eve, although there is nothing recorded on this matter. Adam and Eve knew

Terms of a Will

---

good and evil after they sinned (they ate of the forbidden fruit) in the Garden of Eden. Paul states in the New Testament that he would not have known sin if it had not been for the Ten Commandments. This is food for thought, don't you agree? You can ask Jesus about this when you meet Him.

INHERIT

The word *inherit* is mentioned several times in God's Word. *Inherit* means: To come into possession of something; To receive as a right or title descendible by law from an ancestor at his death.²

Matthew 19:29 promises that you shall *inherit* everlasting life. The promise is to those who forsake all and follow Jesus. Please don't get the idea that you are going to lose something by serving God. There is much to gain.

Matthew 25:34 gives another promise to those who have truly loved God and their neighbor and have served God to the end: *"Inherit* the kingdom prepared for you."

In Mark 10:17 the question was asked by a rich young ruler, "Good Master, what shall I do that I may *inherit* eternal life?" Jesus told him to keep the commandments (verse 19). The six commandments Jesus quoted were concerning how to love his neighbor. The young ruler could not handle the instruction of verse 21, for Jesus said, "Sell what you have, give to the poor, and you will have treasure in heaven: and come, take up the cross, and follow me." The fellow went away sad. He could not give God first place in his life. Jesus knew this before He quoted the commandments, leaving out the first three, which covered placing God first.

Luke 18 gives a slightly different account than Mark 10. "Good Master, what shall I do to *inherit* eternal life?" (Luke 18:18). Jesus answered (verse 20), "Thou knowest the commandments." Luke records Jesus as quoting five commandments, one less than Mark quotes. The commandments are concerning how to love your neighbor as yourself. In verse 21 the young ruler told Jesus that he had kept the commandments from his youth up. Jesus told him (verse 22) he lacked one thing. "Sell all that thou hast, and distribute unto the poor and thou shalt have treasure in heaven: and come, follow me." The fellow's love for money and his failure to keep all the commandments kept him from eternal life.

First Corinthians 6:9 says the unrighteous shall not *inherit* eternal life. The unrighteous includes fornicators (sex before marriage), idolaters, adulterers, the effeminate, abusers of themselves with mankind, thieves, a covetous person, drunkards, revelers, and extortionists. These people shall not *inherit* the kingdom of God. A clearer understanding of these verses may be found in the New International Version of the Bible.

First Corinthians 15:50 says, "Flesh and blood cannot *inherit* the kingdom of God, neither does corruption [perishable] *inherit* incorruption [imperishable]." Verses 51 and 52 explain this mystery: we shall all be changed to incorruptible in the twinkling of an eye. We can have bodies that will not decay, living in a city that will never decay. You can have it if you want it.

Hebrews 6:12 encourages us to not be lazy, but be followers, be patient, and *inherit* the promises.

When Esau would have *inherited* the blessing, he was rejected, because he was a fornicator and one who dishonored God (Hebrews 12:16,17).

First Peter 3:9 tells us not to render evil for evil if we expect to *inherit* a blessing. Verse 10 says to refrain from evil and speak no deceit if we want to see good days. Verse 12 says the face of the Lord is against them that do evil, but the eyes and ears of the Lord are open to the righteous and He will hear their prayers.

> "He that overcometh shall inherit all things; and I will be his God, and he shall be my son."
> Revelation 21:7

INHERITANCE

Inheritance means anything inherited: property, a title, privilege, etc., which passes by law to the heir or is received from predecessors.[1]

Every time I hear the words *inherit, inheritance,* and *heir*, I think again how fortunate I am to have learned the *Will of God.* If only I could find greater and more wonderful words to express my thanks to the Father God for His love given to me through Jesus and the Holy Spirit! Oh, for a thousand tongues to sing, my great Redeemer's love! Even a thousand tongues could not express my thanks.

Jesus made a very stern statement in Matthew 21:43. The kingdom of God can be taken away from you and given to a nation bringing forth fruits. These people lost that which could have been an eternal *inheritance.*

> "And now, brethren, I commend you to God, and to the word of his grace, which is able to build you up, and to give you an *inheritance* among all them which are sanctified."
>
> Acts 20:32

Ephesians 1:11-14 says we have obtained an *inheritance* through the Will of God and after you believed, you were sealed with the Holy Spirit of promise, which is the earnest (pledge) of our *inheritance.*

> "Giving thanks unto the Father, which hath made us meet [fit] to be partakers of the *inheritance* of the saints in light: Who hath delivered us from the power of darkness, and hath translated us into the kingdom of his dear Son."
>
> Colossians 1:12,13

Hebrews 9:15 tells us Jesus is the mediator of the New Testament, and through this *Will* we have received salvation, and so have the Old Testament saints. By His death, they who are called can receive the promise of an eternal *inheritance*.

"To an *inheritance* incorruptible, and undefiled, and that fadeth not away, reserved in heaven for you, Who are kept by the power of God through faith unto salvation ready to be revealed in the last time."

1 Peter 1:4

RANSOM

Ransom: The redemption of a prisoner, slave, captured goods, etc., for a price; the price paid or demanded before a captive is set free; a means of delivering or rescuing, as from sin or its consequences.[1]

Without exception there is a *price* for everything, including a will. In this case, the *price* Jesus paid for your gift, the *Will of God*, was extremely high. His death, terrible as it was, was the *price* paid to set the captives (Old Testament saints) free, and they shall rise from the dead. It was the *price* paid for you and me that we also can enjoy the benefits of belonging to the family of God. There is no greater love than this. My Creator laid down His life so that I can be a part of His family. The Creator became my Savior and I shall live eternally grateful. He can be your Savior too. The choice is yours.

The Son of man, Jesus, gave His life as a *ransom* for many. Jesus' life was the *price* paid to bring about the *Will of God*. He has done this for you, and it is for you, if you will only accept and do His wonderful *Will* (Matthew 20:28 and Mark 10:45).

When Jesus was lifted up on the cross, He was the *ransom* (*price*) that was paid for our eternal life (John 3:14).

> "That whosoever believeth in him should not perish, but have eternal life."
>
> John 3:15

"What! Know ye not that your body is the temple of the Holy Ghost which is in you, which ye have of God, and ye are not your own? For ye are *bought* with a *price*: therefore glorify God in your

body, and in your spirit, which are God's."
1 Corinthians 6:19,20

First Timothy 2:4 tells us all men can be saved and can come into the knowledge of truth. "For there is one God, and one mediator between God and men, the man Christ Jesus; Who gave himself a *ransom* for all" (verses 5 and 6). I feel that the word *truth* (verse 4) spoken of here is the Holy Spirit. The Holy Spirit is the Spirit of Truth, for John 16:13 says when the Spirit of Truth is come, He will guide you into all truth. Jesus is making it known that if He leaves this world, He will send the Comforter (see verse 7). The Comforter is the Holy Spirit and the Spirit of Truth.

A very heavy *price* was paid for the wonderful privilege of being able to say, "I accept and thank You, Lord Jesus, with a grateful heart for the precious and generous *Will of God*."

WILL

We have discussed the word *testament* and its definition. Now let us take a look at the word *will* and its definition. The word has several definitions. The one we are concerned with is with reference to law. Basically, it is the same definition as the word *testament*.

> *Will:* Law; a legal statement of a person's wishes about what shall be done with his property after he is dead; the written document containing such a statement; (formerly) a statement of a person's wishes regarding the disposal of his real property after his death, his personal property being disposed of by testament.[1]

You may be amazed at the number of times the *Will of God* is mentioned in the Bible. I shall attempt to bring out all that will pertain to God's last *Will* and Testament (as the definition reads).

In Matthew 7:21 Jesus states, "Not everyone that saith unto me, Lord, Lord, shall enter the kingdom of heaven." The only people who will make it to the kingdom of heaven are those who know and do the *Will of God*.

> "Many will say to me in that day, Lord, Lord, have we not prophesied in thy name? and in thy name have cast out devils? and in thy name done many wonderful works? And then will I profess unto them, I never knew you: depart from me, ye that work iniquity [unjust, wicked sinners]."
>
> Matthew 7:22,23

Who are Jesus' true kin? Jesus asked the question in Matthew 12:48, then answers His own question in verse 49:

Terms of a Will

"And he stretched forth his hand toward his disciples, and said, Behold my mother and my brethren! For whosoever shall do the will of my Father which is in heaven, the same is my brother, and sister, and mother."
Matthew 12:49,50

In Matthew 21:31, Jesus asked which of a certain man's two sons did the *will* of his father. Read the verses beginning with verse 28 to fill in the story. If you know what the *Will of God* is, you can better understand what Jesus was saying. If you have told the Lord that you will not work for Him, but will repent and go (work) you will have done the *Will of God*. You will have started your eternal journey. If you are to be saved, you must repent and do as God is asking you to do.

As Jesus agonized in prayer in the Garden knowing the pain and grief He would be suffering on the cross, He asked the Father if it were possible, if there could be some other way other than giving His life on the cross (Matthew 26:39). The *Will of God* was to give His only Son that we might be able to receive adoption as sons and daughters with the promise of eternal life as heirs by the new *Will of God*. His Will also provides that we no longer need to sacrifice an animal for forgiveness of sin. Jesus said in verse 39, *"Not as I will*, but as thou wilt." In verse 42 Jesus said again, *"Thy will* be done." Look also at Mark 14:36.

"For whosoever shall do the will of God, the same is my brother, and my sister, and mother."
Mark 3:35

The story of the birth of Jesus states:

"Glory to God in the highest, and on earth peace,

God's Will

good will toward men."
Luke 2:14

Jesus is the Prince of Peace (Isaiah 9:6), inner peace that can come only through Jesus. I feel that the word *good* refers to God. Jesus tells us there is none good but one and that is God. Thus, God's *Will* toward men.

In Acts 22:6-16 Paul is telling the Jews, the Roman captain, soldiers, and centurions about his conversion. In verse 12 He tells of Ananias who came to Saul that he, Saul, should know the *Will of God*.

> "The God of our fathers hath chosen thee, that thou shouldest know his will."
> Acts 22:14

According to verse 15, Paul was to be a witness to all men. Verse 16 states, "Arise, and be baptized, and wash away thy sins, calling on the name of the Lord."

Paul states in Romans 1:9 that he is praying without ceasing for his Roman friends.

> "Making request, if by any means now at length I might have a prosperous journey by the *will of God* to come unto you. For I long to see you, that I may impart unto you some spiritual gift, to the end ye may be established."
> Romans 1:10,11

Romans 8:27 tells us the Spirit makes intercession for the saints according to the *Will of God*.

Romans 12:1 encourages us to be holy. "Be ye transformed by the renewing of your mind, that ye may prove what is that good, and acceptable, and perfect, *will of God*."

Paul says in Romans 15 he hopes to visit Rome. In verse

30 he is asking for their prayers.

> "That I may come unto you with joy by the *will of God*, and may with you be refreshed."
> Romans 15:32

> "Paul, called to be an apostle [called out one] of Jesus Christ through the *will of God* . . ."
> 1 Corinthians 1:1

> "Paul, an apostle of Jesus Christ by the *will of God* . . ."
> 2 Corinthians 1:1

> "Our sufficiency is of God; Who also hath made us able ministers of the new testament; not of the letter, but of the spirit: for the letter killeth, but the spirit giveth life."
> 2 Corinthians 3:5,6

"And this they did . . . gave their own selves to the Lord, and unto us by the *will* of God" (2 Corinthians 8:5). Paul is speaking here of the churches of Macedonia: how they gave generously, even at a time of poverty. They not only gave their money, but also themselves to support the work.

In Galatians 1:1 Paul is greeting the churches at Galatia. In verse 4 he tells them that Jesus gave himself as a sacrifice (speaking of His death) for our sins that He might deliver us from this present evil world, according to the *Will of God* and our Father.

In Ephesians 1 Paul teaches that the adoption as children of God (adoption through the Will of God) was predestinated by Jesus Christ.

> "Having predestinated us unto the adoption of

God's Will

children by Jesus Christ to himself, according to the good pleasure of his will."

Ephesians 1:5

Yes, the *Will of God* was predestinated. Praise God! Anyone can become a child of God by accepting and doing this wonderful *Will of God*.

"Having made known unto us the mystery of his will, according to his good pleasure which he hath purposed in himself."

Ephesians 1:9

"In whom also we have obtained an inheritance, being predestinated according to the purpose of him who worketh all things after the counsel of his own *will*."

Ephesians 1:11

The *Will of God* was predestinated by the Father God, with Jesus Christ (God the Son) as mediator.

"Wherefore he saith, Awake thou that sleepest, and arise from the dead, and Christ shall give thee light. See then that ye walk circumspectly [as though you were children of Abraham, proud but cautious] not as fools, but as wise . . . be not unwise, but understanding what the *will* of the Lord is . . . be filled with the Spirit; Speaking to yourselves in psalms and hymns and spiritual songs, singing and making melody in your heart to the Lord."

Ephesians 5:14-19

"Giving thanks always for all things unto God and

the Father in the name of our Lord Jesus Christ."
Ephesians 5:20

Ephesians 6:6 tells us to serve the Lord, "Not with eyeservice, as men pleasers; but as the servants of Christ, doing the will of God from the heart."

Philippians 2:13 says, "For it is God which worketh in you both to *will* and to do of his good pleasure." Note that the writer has made known two different definitions of the word *will*. The first Will is *law*, referring to the *Will* Jesus brought through His death on the cross. The second Will is referring to His good pleasure, or doing things that are pleasing in God's sight. I feel it is very important to recognize the two meanings.

> "For this cause we also, since the day we heard it, do not cease to pray for you, and to desire that ye might be filled with the knowledge of his will in all wisdom and spiritual understanding."
> Colossians 1:9

In Colossians 4:12 Paul says that "Epaphras, who is one of you," is praying fervently "that ye may stand perfect and complete in all the *will of God*."

In 1 Thessalonians 4 Paul teaches that your sanctification is the *Will* of God.

> "For this is the will of God, even your sanctification, that ye should abstain from fornication . . . For God hath not called us unto uncleanness, but unto holiness."
> 1 Thessalonians 4:3,7

> "Rejoice evermore. Pray without ceasing. In every thing give thanks: for this is the will of God in

God's Will

Christ Jesus concerning you. Quench not the Spirit. Despise not prophesyings. Prove all things; hold fast that which is good. Abstain from all appearance of evil. And the very God of peace sanctify you wholly; and I pray God your whole spirit and soul and body be preserved blameless unto the coming of our Lord Jesus Christ."
1 Thessalonians 5:16-23

Paul sends a personal greeting to Timothy in 2 Timothy 1:1,2:

"Paul, an apostle of Jesus Christ by the will of God, according to the promise of life which is in Christ Jesus, To Timothy, my dearly beloved son."
2 Timothy 1:1,2

"God also bearing them witness, both with signs and wonders, and with divers [various] miracles, and gifts of the Holy Ghost, according to his own *will*."
Hebrews 2:4

The word *testament* is mentioned six times in Hebrews 9:15-20. *Testator* is mentioned in verses 16 and 17. The section of Scripture in Hebrews 9:11-28 is probably the most important Scripture of all to help you completely understand the *Will of God*. If you have studied the Scriptures given you thus far, you should be able to step into these verses with understanding. Read these verses several times so that they become perfectly clear to you.

Jesus, God's Son, the perfect Lamb of God, the perfect blood sacrifice for the redemption of man, was offered once, on the cross, and there will be no other blood sacrifice for the forgiveness of sin, thus replacing the old *Will of God*

Terms of a Will

with the New Will of God. The first *Will* is now in place and valid for all the Old Testament saints. The only hope of eternal life for all who have lived since Jesus' death is through the New *Will of God*. Hebrews 9:22 says, "Without shedding of blood there is no remission" of sins. Without the death of Jesus, both *Wills, Old* and *New*, would still be the promised *Will* in print only. Verse 24 tells us Christ is not entered into the holy places made with hands, but is in heaven sitting at the right hand of God, hearing your prayers and making intercession on your behalf to the Father God. Imagine that! God the Son, taking your prayers and pleading to the Father God on your behalf. Fantastic! Can you now see how important you are in God's sight? Remember that God is love, He is the source of love, and without Him there is no love. Love is only an emotion without God.

Jesus the Son of God has suffered much as He watched man sin since the beginning of His creation. His heart has been broken unnumbered times because of sin. He has watched man weep and cry over the results of sin and now in the end time, has given himself once to die by the sacrifice of himself. Can you imagine how God has wept over the tears man has shed? He was willing to give up His only Son in an effort to get you and me to see how much He cares for us and show us how sin will destroy an individual. All men will die and will face judgment. I am so glad that I have Jesus to be my judge, because He lived here on earth and He knows the weakness of man. He became man that He might better understand us. He is my best friend and He can be your best friend also. Jesus will return again and lead us into eternity, never to die again, if we know and do His *Will*.

Did you ever wonder why God would want to do away with animal sacrifice and give His only Son to die? Why not continue the blood sacrifice of animals? The reason: There was no real change in the people and the sacrifice became a ritual. The sacrifice of animals was made as an act of faith for the forgiveness of sins. I wonder if the *Old Testament* saints really understood that the blood of bulls and goats could not take away sins, that God himself would have to come to earth and shed His blood and die in order to validate the written *Will of God*? There are still many who do not understand this, but hopefully this book will reveal the mystery.

The most important point here is this: There must be the death of one making a *will* in order that the heir can receive the benefits of the *will*.

Hebrews 10:1 makes it obvious that the *Old Will* sacrifices did not make or cause man to become perfect. If it had, they would have ceased to offer animals (verse 2). Verse 4 states that the offering of bulls and goats will not take away sins. Verses 5-7 repeat the Old Testament promise found in Psalm 40:6-8 and of the *Will of God* that was to come and is now here. Read these verses in Hebrews, then read Psalm 40.

In Hebrews 10:7 Jesus said, "I come . . . to do thy *will* O God." Verse 9 tells us He took away the *Old Will* to establish the second or *New Will* of God. By the same Will we are sanctified once and for all (verse 10). The word *all* means that sanctification is for both Jew and Gentile, through the offering of the body of Jesus.

> "For ye have need of patience, that, after ye have done the will of God, ye might receive the promise."
>
> Hebrews 10:36

The promise is "the reward of your inheritance" (Colossians 3:24).

> "Now the just shall live by faith: but if any man draw back, my soul shall have no pleasure in him. But we are not of them who draw back unto perdi-

Terms of a Will

tion [the loss of one's soul or the joys of heaven; final spiritual ruin; damnation]; but of them that believe to the saving of the soul."
Hebrews 10:38,39

Hebrews 12:24 says, "Jesus is the mediator of the new *covenant* [testament]."

"Now the God of peace, that brought again from the dead our Lord Jesus, that great shepherd of the sheep, through the blood of the everlasting *covenant* [testament], Make you perfect in every good work to do his *will*, working in you that which is well-pleasing in his sight, through Jesus Christ; to whom be glory for ever and ever. Amen."
Hebrews 13:20,21

"Christ hath suffered for us in the flesh, arm yourselves likewise with the same mind: for he that suffered in the flesh hath ceased from sin."
1 Peter 4:1

"That he no longer should live the rest of his time in the flesh to the lusts of men, but to the *will of God*."
1 Peter 4:2

"What shall be the end of them that obey not the gospel of God? And if the righteous scarcely be saved, where shall the ungodly and the sinner appear? Wherefore, let them that suffer according to the will of God commit the keeping of their souls to him in well doing, as unto a faithful Creator."
1 Peter 4:17-19

God's Will

A sinner is one who deliberately breaks one of the Ten Commandments (see 1 John 3:4). But who are the ungodly? The late Reverend Guy Slate, a very dear friend of mine, told me that he felt the ungodly are those who hang around the church, claiming to be Christians, opposing everything good, backbiting, faultfinding, criticizing, and bearing false witness against their neighbor, and all the time trying to build themselves up by putting others down.

Is there any difference between the sinner and the ungodly? A hint is in Mark 12:29-31: Love God with all your heart, soul, mind, and strength and love your neighbor as yourself. It seems to me that the ungodly and sinners are in the same mess. Neither will inherit eternal life.

First John 2:15 tells us, "Love not the world, neither the things that are in the world." If you love worldly things, the love of the Father is not in you. Verse 16 says, "The lust of the flesh, and the lust of the eyes, and the pride of life, is not of the Father, but is of the world."

> "And the world passeth away, and the lust thereof: but he that doeth the will of God abideth forever."
> 1 John 2:17

First John 5:14 says if we ask Christ for anything He hears us, *if* we ask according to His *Will*. God will answer your prayer if your prayer is not self-centered, if it is right in God's sight, and the best for everyone concerned.

We have covered a lot of Scriptures concerning the word *will* as in the *Will of God*. I trust it has been enlightening and enjoyable.

Now we will move on to the last two words in our study on terms of a *will* and look at some Scriptures concerning those terms.

REDEEM

Christ came to redeem. *Redeem:* To make good, carry out, fulfill. We redeem a promise when we do what we say we will do. To set free; rescue; save; to be redeemed from sin.[1]

"... the great God and our Savior Jesus Christ; Who gave himself for us, that he might redeem us from all iniquity, and purify unto himself a peculiar people, zealous of good works."
Titus 2:13,14

Jesus *made good* His promise (Will) to us, by giving up His life. Through this *Will* we are set free, rescued or saved from sin, unto eternal salvation.

"But when the fullness of the time was come, God sent forth his Son, made of a woman, made under the law, To redeem them that were under the law, that we might receive the adoption of sons. And because ye are sons, God hath sent forth the Spirit of his Son into your hearts, crying, Abba, Father. Wherefore thou art no more a servant, but a son; and if a son, then an heir of God through Christ."
Galatians 4:4-7

REDEMPTION

Redemption: Redeeming; being redeemed; deliverance; rescue; deliverance from sin; salvation.[1]

Zechariah was filled with the Holy Ghost, and prophesied after he had regained his ability to speak (Luke 1:67).

> "Blessed be the Lord God of Israel; for he hath visited and redeemed his people, And hath raised up an horn of salvation for us in the house of his servant David . . . To perform the mercy promised to our fathers, and to remember his holy covenant; The oath which he swore to our father Abraham."
>
> Luke 1:68,69,72,73

Luke 2:25-35 tells about Simeon, a just and devout man, one filled with the Holy Ghost. The Holy Ghost revealed to him that he would not see death until he would see the Lord's Christ. Led by the Spirit, he went into the temple when the parents brought Jesus in to be circumcised. Simeon took the child Jesus into his arms and blessed God and said:

> "Lord, now lettest thou thy servant depart in peace, according to thy word: For mine eyes have seen thy salvation, Which thou hast prepared before the face of all people; A light to lighten the Gentiles, and the glory of thy people Israel."
>
> Luke 2:29-32

Simeon also prophesied of Jesus' fall (death) and rising again. He told Mary that a sword would pierce her soul also.

Luke 2:36-38 tells about Anna, a prophetess, probably over one hundred years old, who served in the temple, fast-

Terms of a Will

ing and praying night and day.

> "And she coming in that instant gave thanks likewise unto the Lord, and spake of him to all them that looked for redemption in Jerusalem."
> Luke 2:38

The verses in Luke 21:25-28 speak of the second coming of the Son of man, Jesus Christ. "There shall be signs in the sun, and in the moon, and in the stars; and upon the earth distress of nations, with perplexity: the sea and the waves roaring; Men's hearts failing them for fear, and looking after those things which are coming on the earth: for the powers of heaven shall be shaken."

> "And then shall they see the Son of man coming in a cloud with power and great glory. And when these things begin to come to pass, then look up, and lift up your heads; for your redemption draweth nigh."
> Luke 21:27,28

The two men on the road to Emmaus talked with Jesus but failed to recognize Him. They spoke of Jesus' crucifixion and said:

> "But we trusted that it had been he which should have redeemed Israel: and beside all this, today is the third day since these things were done."
> Luke 24:21

The third day was the day the Lord was to have risen from the dead.

"For all have sinned, and come short of the glory

God's Will

of God; Being justified freely by his grace through the redemption that is in Christ Jesus."

Romans 3:23,24

In 1 Corinthians 1, Paul warns against divisions and not thinking of ourselves more highly than we should. Only God the Father through Jesus Christ is the source of strength, and without the Father and the Son man would be without wisdom, righteousness, sanctification, and *redemption* (salvation).

> "But of him are ye in Christ Jesus, who of God is made unto us wisdom, and righteousness, and sanctification, and redemption: That, according as it is written, He that glorieth, let him glory in the Lord."
>
> 1 Corinthians 1:30,31

Abraham received God's covenant (Will) by faith, not by the law (Galatians 3:6,7). Righteousness was accounted to Abraham because of his faith, and they which are of faith are the same as children of Abraham.

> "Christ hath redeemed us from the curse of the law, being made a curse for us: for it is written, Cursed is every one that hangeth on a tree: That the blessing of Abraham might come on the Gentiles through Jesus Christ; that we might receive the promise of the Spirit through faith."
>
> Galatians 3:13,14

What are the blessings of Abraham? That's right, it is the wonderful *Will of God*. The Old *Will* of God was given to Abraham by promise, not by the law (Galatians 3:18). Abraham accepted the *Will* by faith. We accept the *New Will of God* by faith the same way Abraham received the Old Will of God.

We have *redemption* (salvation from sin, and from the soul's eternal punishment) through the blood (or death) of Jesus Christ, for the forgiveness of sins, according to the riches of His grace (Ephesians 1:7).

> "See then that ye walk circumspectly, not as fools, but as wise, Redeeming the time, because the days are evil. Wherefore be ye not unwise, but understanding what the will of the Lord is."
> Ephesians 5:15-17

Jesus has, by giving His life, obtained eternal *redemption* (salvation) for us. Bringing *redemption* (salvation) for those who are under the first *testament* (Old Will of God) that they which are called might receive the promise of an eternal inheritance (Hebrews 9:12,15).

Jesus is the mediator of the *New Testament*, and by this *Will*, we are *all* included (Hebrews 10:9,10).

You were not *redeemed* with corruptible things such as silver or gold, or from your vain conversation handed down from your fathers (1 Peter 1:18).

> "But with the precious blood of Christ, as of a lamb without blemish and without spot: Who verily was foreordained before the foundation of the world, but was manifest in these last times for you."
> 1 Peter 1:19,20

There is only one worthy of opening the seven seals of the book of tribulations. That one is He (Jesus) who has *redeemed* us to God by His blood. It is for every kindred, tongue, people, and nation (Revelation 5:9).

Revelation 14:1-3 tells of the 144,000 which were *redeemed*, the firstfruits unto God and to the Lamb.

> "These are they which were not defiled with women; for they are virgins. These are they which follow the Lamb whithersoever he goeth. These were redeemed from among men, being the firstfruits unto God and to the Lamb. And in their mouth was found no guile: for they are without fault before the throne of God."
>
> Revelation 14:4,5

Chapter 3

Summary

This chapter has been a study of words relating to a *will* or *testament,* confirming that we are actually talking about a *will.*

Testament is a will. *Testator* is the person making a will. *Heir* is one who receives property or title after the death of the testator. *Inherit* is to receive as a right or title descendible by law from an ancestor at his death. *Inheritance* means anything inherited. *Ransom* is the price paid for our eternal gift. *Redeem* is to make good a promise. *Redemption* is deliverance from sin—salvation.

CHAPTER 4

THE NEW WILL OF GOD

The *Will of God* was always a mystery to me, until one day at church a lady told a story of another lady who was blaming God for the death of her child. She had prayed for the child to recover from an illness, but the child died. This really troubled me, so I began searching the Bible to discover just what the *Will of God* really is. I asked myself these questions: *Is God's Will something that will always be a mystery? Can I know for sure what the Will of God is?*

Believe me, if you sincerely want to know what the *Will of God* is, you must first ask God for wisdom and knowledge, both of which are gifts of the Holy Spirit (1 Corinthians 12:8). This is exactly what I did and now I know His *Will*. It is now my pleasure to share with you what God has shared with me.

When you complete this study you should know why the child was not healed.

We will now take the *Will of God* one section at a time, starting with the Preamble, explain it, then move on to the next part.

THE WILL OF GOD
PREAMBLE

To all who repent of their sins and believe that I am the only true and living God, I, God the Father, God the Son, and God the Holy Spirit, do will the following:

The *Will* is to all and for all who will accept it and do it, but this Preamble is very hard for some people to accept.

Did you ever try to say you were sorry for something you may have said or done, and you felt that if you said it your jaw would surely break? Then you finally said it, "I'm so sorry," and wow! What a relief! You feel as though you were a balloon that had been blown up so tight you would almost burst, then the air is released. Whisssssh, whirling around and around the room and now lying on the floor, air totally gone, tension gone, you feel so limp and relaxed you almost feel as though the world had suddenly jumped off your shoulders.

To say "I'm sorry" or to repent should not be that difficult. Don't let yourself get caught in this trap for it could mean you will miss everlasting life.

Many people have experienced this same feeling when they made the decision to follow Jesus. But to ask forgiveness was really tough. I remember very well how hard it was for me. I was so under conviction for things done in the past, but refusing to repent I would hold onto the church pew in front of me until my knuckles turned white, because I was afraid to repent. Years passed before I finally gave in and repented of my sins. Thank God I lived long enough to see forgiveness.

Why is repentance so tough? Satan, the prince and power of the air, deceives us. He goes about roaring like a lion seeking whom he may devour. It is sad to say, but we all underestimate the power of Satan. Let us learn early in life to ask forgiveness and not let an unforgiving spirit deprive us of an eternal inheritance. Learn to repent. A hateful, unforgiving attitude can even be harmful to our minds and bodies.

REPENT

To receive the *Will of God*, you must *repent* and believe. *Repent* is a word often used, but do we really know what it means? The word *repent* means: To feel sorry for sin and seek forgiveness; regret something done in the past.[1]

The Bible tells us many times to *repent*. *Repent* of what? We are to *repent* of our sins (Matthew 3:2). John the Baptist taught that all people should *repent* for the kingdom of heaven is at hand. Jesus himself preached the same message (Matthew 4:7).

Jesus began preaching the good news of the kingdom of God saying, "*Repent* ye, and believe the gospel" (Mark 1:15). The twelve disciples preached that men should *repent* (Mark 6:12).

Jesus said, "Except ye *repent,* ye shall all likewise perish" (Luke 13:3). He meant that they will not inherit eternal life. In Luke 16:19-31, Jesus is telling a parable of a rich man in hell begging that someone be sent to his five brothers from the grave. But Abraham replied:

> "They have Moses and the prophets; let them hear them. And he said, Nay, father Abraham: but if one went unto them from the dead, they will repent. And he said unto him, If they hear not Moses and the prophets, neither will they be persuaded, though one rose from the dead."
> Luke 16:29-31

In Luke 17 Jesus teaches that if your brother trespasses against you, you should confront him and if he will *repent*, forgive him. Verse 4 says even if he trespasses seven times a day, if he should *repent*, you must forgive him.

"Peter said unto them, *Repent,* and be baptized

every one of you in the name of Jesus Christ for the remission of sins, and ye shall receive the gift of the Holy Ghost. For the promise is unto you, and to your children, and to all that are afar off, even as many as the Lord our God shall call."
Acts 2:38,39

The word *all* includes both you and me. *Repent* and be converted, that your sins may be blotted out (Acts 3:19). *Repent* for your wickedness (Acts 8:22). God commanded all men to *repent* (Acts 17:30). And that they (the Gentiles) should *repent* and turn to God and do good works meet for *repentance* (Acts 26:20).

All the following verses speak of *repentance* and what to expect if you don't *repent*: Revelation 2:5,16,21,22; 3:3,19.

Even the devil believes that Jesus is the Son of God, but he has no desire to *repent* of sin.

> *Repent* . . . what do you have to lose? Hell and the lake of fire.
> *Repent* . . . what do you have to gain? Eternal life and paradise.

Repentance is the first step to receiving the *Will* of God.

BELIEVE

The word *believe* is defined: To have faith; trust; to be convinced of the actual existence, occurrence, validity, or truth of something; to have religious belief; to exercise faith: "Be not afraid, only *believe*" (Mark 5:36).[1]

"The time is fulfilled, and the kingdom of God is at hand: repent ye, and *believe* the gospel" (Mark 1:15).

> "He that *believeth* and is baptized shall be saved; but he that *believeth* not shall be damned. And these signs shall follow them that *believe*; In my name shall they cast out devils; they shall speak with new tongues; They shall take up serpents; and if they drink any deadly thing, it shall not hurt them; they shall lay hands on the sick, and they shall recover."
>
> Mark 16:16-18

In the Book of Luke, chapter 8, Jesus is explaining the parable (story) of the sower to His disciples, for they did not understand.

> "And he said, Unto you it is given to know the mysteries of the kingdom of God: but to others in parables . . . "
>
> Luke 8:10

In verse 11 He explained that the seed is the Word of God. Some will receive it, and the devil will take it away lest they *believe* and be saved. Some will receive it with joy, and having no roots, will *believe* for awhile, and when temptation comes along, they will fall away (verse 13).

The New Will of God

> "But as many as received him, to them gave he power to become the sons of God, even to them that believe on his name: Which were born, not of blood, nor of the will of the flesh, nor of the will of man, but of God."
>
> John 1:12,13

Yes! By the *Will* of God. God loved the world so much, He gave His only Son to be the last blood sacrifice for the forgiveness of sin, and bring about the *Will of God* for all who *believe*. No one should perish, if they will receive His *Will* and do it (John 3:15-18). If you would like to receive everlasting life, you must *believe* on the Son or else receive the wrath of God (John 3:36).

> "And Jesus said unto them, I am the bread of life: he that cometh to me shall never hunger; and he that believeth on me shall never thirst . . . And this is the will of him that sent me, that every one which seeth the Son, and believeth on him, may have everlasting life: and I will raise him up at the last day."
>
> John 6:35,40

> "He that believeth on me, as the scripture hath said, out of his belly shall flow rivers of living water."
>
> John 7:38

Here Jesus was speaking of the Spirit who was to come, for the Holy Ghost was not yet given. In John 8:23,24 Jesus explains that if you do not believe He is from above you will die in you sins. In John 10:25 Jesus said, "I told you and ye *believed* not" (this He said in answer to the question as to whether he was the Christ).

God's Will

"But ye believe not, because ye are not of my sheep, as I said unto you. My sheep hear my voice, and I know them, and they follow me."
John 10:26,27

Search the following Scriptures on the words *believe, believeth,* and *believed:* John 11:25,26,40,45; John 12:44,46; Romans 1:16; Romans 10:4,9,10,11,14; 1 John 5:1,10,13.

BELIEVE JESUS IS THE SON OF GOD

Many people believe that Jesus was a terrific teacher. He had great wisdom and understanding, yet they did not believe He was the *Son of God*, let alone, God the Son.

Read the Scriptures to help you understand who Jesus was and is. Remember, even the devil believed that Jesus was the *Son of God*. In order to receive the *Will of God* you must receive and do the entire *Will*. No part can be left out. If you fully understand His *Will*, you will not want to leave out any part.

In order to understand what God himself actually gave up in order that we might have eternal life, read the Scriptures pertaining to His *Son* Jesus. Before we start, ask yourself this question: *Would I, if I could, be willing to give up my son that my neighbor could have the gift of eternal life?*

Matthew 3:17 tells us that a voice from heaven said, "This is my beloved *Son*." How many voices from heaven have you heard? You can assume it must have been God the Father who spoke. Jesus is the *Son of God*. Matthew 8:29 says that even the demons recognize who Jesus is. They called Him the *Son of God*. Matthew 11:27 says no one knows the *Son of God*, except it be revealed by the Father, neither does anyone know the Father, except it be revealed to him by the *Son*, Jesus.

After seeing Jesus and Peter walk on the water, the disciples said, "Of a truth thou art the Son of God" (Matthew 14:33).

Peter acknowledged that Jesus was the *Son of God* (Matthew 16:16). A voice from a cloud overhead spoke, "This is my beloved *Son*" (Matthew 17:5). In Matthew 26:63,64, Jesus admits He is the *Son of God* and says He will be sitting at the right hand of God. "For he said, I am the *Son of God*" (Matthew 27:43).

"When the centurion, and they that were with him, watching Jesus [crucifixion], saw the earthquake, and those things that were done, they feared greatly, saying, Truly this was the *Son of God*."
Matthew 27:54

Mark 1:1 says, "The beginning of the gospel of Jesus Christ the *Son of God* . . . " Read also the following Scriptures concerning Jesus, the *Son of God:* Mark 1:11, 3:11, 5:7, 9:7, 14:61,62, and 15:39; Luke 1:32,35, 3:22, 8:28, 10:22, 22:70; John 1:34,49, 3:18,35,36, 8:38; Romans 1:3,4, 8:32; 1 John 5:1,10,11,12,13.

If you believe the Bible is true, you have here all the Scriptures you need to make a logical decision as to the fact that Jesus is the *Son of God*.

The next logical step then is to *believe* that Jesus is God the Son. Can you believe this? Let us move on into the next section as I give you plenty of Scriptures concerning God the Son.

The New Will of God

BELIEVE THAT JESUS IS GOD THE SON

"Behold, a virgin shall conceive, and bear a son, and shall call his name *Immanuel* [God with us]" (Isaiah 7:14). This is a prophecy concerning the coming of our Lord and Savior, Jesus Christ.

Matthew 1:23, speaking of Jesus, says, "They shall call his name *Emmanuel*, which being interpreted is, *God with us*." This is prophecy fulfilled.

> "For the Son of man is Lord even of the sabbath day."
> Matthew 12:8

I find this very interesting since the third commandment reads: "Thou shalt not take the name of the *Lord thy God* in vain" (Exodus 20:7). *The Lord is God.* Thus, *God the Son.* Matthew 23:39 says, "Blessed is he that cometh in the name of the *Lord*."

Mark 2:28 says Jesus, "The Son of man is *Lord* also of the Sabbath." Mark 12:29,30 says, "The *Lord* our *God* is one *Lord:* And thou shalt love the *Lord* thy *God* with all thy heart, and with all thy soul, and with all thy mind, and with all thy strength."

> "Blessed, *be* the *Lord God* of Israel; for he [Jesus] hath visited and redeemed his people."
> Luke 1:68

> "For unto you is born this day in the city of David a Savior, which is Christ the Lord."
> Luke 2:11

> "In the beginning was the Word, and the Word was with God, and the Word was God. The same was

God's Will

in the beginning with God. All things were made by him; and without him was not any thing made that was made. In him was life; and the life was the light of men . . . He was in the world, and the world was made by him, and the world knew him not."

John 1:1-4,10

The *Lord God* made the earth and the heavens (Genesis 2:4). "The *Lord God* formed man of the dust" (Genesis 2:7). "The *Lord God* planted the Garden of Eden" (Genesis 2:8). "The *Lord God* made the trees to grow" (Genesis 2:9). "The *Lord God* made woman" (Genesis 2:18). "The *Lord God* formed every beast and fowl" (Genesis 2:19).

"I am come in my Father's name, and ye receive me not: if another shall come in his own name, him ye will receive."

John 5:43

"Jesus said unto them, Verily, verily, I say unto you, Before Abraham was, *I am*."

John 8:58

God told Moses to tell the children of Israel, *I AM* sent you (Exodus 3:14). *I AM is God*. Jesus is *I AM*.

Peter called Him (Jesus) Lord (John 13:6) and Jesus answered,

"Ye call me Master and Lord: and ye say well; for so I am."

John 13:13

"And Thomas answered and said unto him, My Lord and my God."

John 20:28

In John 17:11 Jesus prayed that His followers may be one as *He, Jesus, and God are one*. Did you ever think that you could be one as Jesus and God are one? You can be, by doing the total *Will of God*.

Acts 2:36 says God has made Jesus both *Lord and Christ*.

In Romans 1:3 Paul refers to Jesus Christ as "our *Lord*." Remember, the *Lord* is God. Verse 4 says Jesus was "declared to be the Son of God," thus *God the Son*.

"But to us there is but one God, the *Father* . . . and one *Lord Jesus Christ*" (1 Corinthians 8:6). The third commandment states, "Thou shalt not take the name of the *Lord* thy God in vain" (Exodus 20:7). I have to conclude that Jesus our *Lord* wrote the Ten Commandments, but remember this: Jesus came to do the *Will* of the Father. Jesus wrote that which the Father commanded Him.

The Father God, through Jesus, created all things (Ephesians 3:9). "In the beginning *God* created the heavens and the earth" (Genesis 1:1). Thus, *God the Son*.

Colossians 1:15 refers to Jesus as "the image of the invisible *God*, the firstborn of every creature." Verse 16 says all things were created by Him; thus, *God the Son*. "He is before all things, and by him all things consist" (verse 17).

Jesus in the beginning laid the foundations of the earth. *He is called Lord*. The heavens are also the works of His hands. The *Lord is God* (Hebrews 1:10).

"[Jesus] will be to them a *God*, and they shall be to me a people" (Hebrews 8:10). Jesus is speaking here of the new covenant (Will) with the house of Israel.

"There are three that bear record in heaven, the *Father*, the *Word [Jesus]*, and the *Holy Ghost:* and these three are one" (1 John 5:7). *All are God*.

You can clearly see that Jesus is *God the Son*, as well as the *Son of God*. I hope that you can accept this second step into the *Will of God*. Step one: repent; step two: believe in the only true and living God—God the Father, God the Son, and God the Holy Spirit. We are now ready to consider Part One of the *Will of God*.

Chapter 4

Summary

The *New Will* of God is a "done deal." The *Will* has been written, the testator has made it valid. God's Will is for any individual who will by faith, receive it. In order to receive the *Will* you must repent of your sins and believe in the Trinity—God the Father, God the Son, and God the Holy Spirit.

CHAPTER 5

THE WILL OF GOD
PART ONE

I want you to have the finest things that life has to offer. Please accept the guide to a happy, prosperous, healthy, and successful life found in Exodus 20:1-17. These words were written that you might have a better understanding of perfect love for both Me and your neighbor. Know them, for they can keep you from heartbreak and bitter tears in the late hours at night. My love for you is beyond your fullest understanding. Keep these words in your heart that you might know happiness as an individual, a nation, or as a universe.

THE TEN COMMANDMENTS

This part of *the Will of God* is probably the most misunderstood of all the Scriptures God has given mankind. It is the part about the *Ten Commandments* and how they relate to your life.

As we examine Part One of *the Will of God*, let's keep our minds open as well as our Bibles.

How can the *Ten Commandments* relate to: *happy, prosperous, healthy,* and *successful*? One of the greatest thrills in writing this book was to come to a more complete understanding on this subject. The *Ten Commandments* have shown me how to love. I hope that you too can say the same after reading this chapter.

Pause here and pray for wisdom and understanding if you have not already done so. Remember, wisdom and the word of knowledge are yours for the asking. They are gifts of the Holy Spirit (1 Corinthians 12:8, James 1:5).

The Will of God Part One

HAPPY

The word *happy* is mentioned twenty times in the Old Testament and six times in the New Testament (KJV).³

The word *happy* is defined: Having a feeling of or showing pleasure and joy; glad; pleased; contented.¹

The Bible version of *happy* is as follows:

- Job 5:17—Happy is the person whom God corrects.
- Psalm 144:15—Happy is the person whose God is the Lord.
- Proverbs 3:13—Happy is the person who finds wisdom and understanding.
- Proverbs 3:18—Happy is everyone who retains wisdom.
- Proverbs 16:20—Happy is he who trusts in the Lord.
- Proverbs 28:14—Happy is the man who fears the Lord, but he who hardens his heart shall fall into mischief.
- Proverbs 29:18—Happy is he who keeps the law.
- John 13:16,17—Happy is he who is a servant of God and his fellow man, and understands that he is not greater than Jesus, and that Jesus is not greater than His Heavenly Father who sent Him.
- James 5:11—Happy are those who endure, having patience in afflictions, as in the life of Job.
- 1 Peter 3:14—Happy is he who will suffer for righteousness sake.
- 1 Peter 4:14—Happy are you who are criticized for the name of Christ, for the spirit of glory and of God rests on you.

Happiness is placing God first in your life, and loving

your neighbor as yourself, and this speaks of the Ten Commandments.

PROSPEROUS

"Only be thou strong and very courageous, that thou mayest observe to do according to all the law, which Moses my servant commanded thee: turn not from it to the right hand or to the left, that thou mayest *prosper* whithersoever thou goest. This book of the law shall not depart out of thy mouth; but thou shalt meditate therein day and night, that thou mayest observe to do according to all that is written therein: for then thou shalt make thy way *prosperous*, and then thou shalt have good success."

Joshua 1:7,8

"Blessed is the man that walketh not in the counsel of the ungodly, nor standeth in the way of sinners, nor sitteth in the seat of the scornful. But his delight is in the law of the Lord; and in his law doth he meditate day and night. And he shall be like a tree planted by the rivers of water, that bringeth forth his fruit in his season; his leaf also shall not wither; and whatsoever he doeth shall *prosper*."

Psalm 1:1-3

The words *prosperous, prosper, prospereth,* and *prosperity,* seem to relate mostly to the commandments; i.e., keeping the commandments is to succeed spiritually (see 2 Kings 18:6,7; 1 Chronicles 29:19,23; 2 Chronicles 14:4,7, 31:21, 32:30; Ezra 6:14; Job 9:4; Daniel 6:28; Romans 1:10; 3 John 2). God's children seem to prosper when they keep God's commandments. Approximately ninety verses in the Bible refer to this subject. Search them.

HEALTHY

What is *healthy* about keeping the commandments? How about this for a starter. Commandment number four states that we should take one day to rest each week. God knew that man needed a day of rest. He created us, so I believe that He knows. If someone tried to take away our one day of rest, the entire world would rebel. Am I right or wrong? It is *healthy* and right to take one day each week to rest. The body needs it (Exodus 20:8-10).

Would you like your life on earth to be extended? Commandment number five tells you to listen to your father and mother. They have lived longer than you. They have taken several "lumps" themselves and are better able to warn you of trouble ahead. There are many things to shorten your life, listen to your elders. Evaluate what they say and don't be closed minded. Remember, they love you. Your mother went through the jaws of death to bring you into this world, then fed you and put clothes on your back. Your parents have a real investment in you and want the best for you. God really loves you and so do your parents. It is *healthy* to listen to your parents. So honor your father and mother and God promised you will live longer.

If there was no adultery or fornication in this world today and/or in the past, how few venereal diseases and AIDS cases, broken-hearted people, broken homes, weeping children, heart-broken parents, and sad grandparents would there be today? I would venture to say that adultery and fornication has brought more mental anguish and disease to this world than any one single sin man has ever committed.

God tried to tell mankind not to do these things, but a large number of people failed to see the good in His advice.

Is it *healthy* to live as God directs? There is no doubt about it.

SUCCESSFUL LIFE

A *successful life* is understanding that God is love, and that by following His line of reasoning, one day we shall *succeed* in having eternal life. Until then we can enjoy the finest things of this present life if we love Him and keep His commandments.

DESTROY THE TEN COMMANDMENTS?

Some feel the *Ten Commandments* were done away with in the New *Will of God*, but were they? Remember that Jesus wrote the *Ten Commandments*. Let's examine the Word. Jesus said very plainly that He came not to destroy the *Law* but to fulfill the *Law* (Matthew 5:17). The *commandments* have always been love, but very few understood it in this light. Nothing is to be removed from them. Jesus said:

> "For verily I say unto you, Till heaven and earth pass, one jot or one tittle shall in no wise pass from the law, till all be fulfilled. Whosoever therefore shall break one of these least commandments, and shall teach men so, he shall be called the least in the kingdom of heaven: but whosoever shall do and teach them, the same shall be called great in the kingdom of heaven. For I say unto you, That except your righteousness shall exceed the righteousness of the scribes and Pharisees, ye shall in no case enter into the kingdom of heaven."
>
> Matthew 5:18-20

The Creator gave you and me only two abilities when we were born. One was to cry when we needed something, and the other was to take nourishment from our mother. Everything else had to be learned. How can any person say they know right from wrong if they have never been taught? Since Jesus was our Creator, He knew better than anyone else that if He taught the *commandments* to us, we would not bang our heads against the wall of error as many times, trying to find the truth by trial.

Why are the *Ten Commandments* part of the *New Will of God*? The problem of understanding love is the same today as it was then. Jesus said He came not to destroy the (law) *commandments* but to fulfill them, meaning this love is the fulfillment of the law (Romans 13:10). If we keep His *commandments*, love is perfected in us (1 John 2:4,5). So you see, there is really no way we can remove love from the *New Will of God*.

In Matthew 15:4 Jesus quotes the *commandment* to honor our father and mother. But men have changed the commandment of God to suit themselves.

> "This people draweth nigh unto me with their mouth, and honoreth me with their lips; but their heart is far from me. But in vain they do worship me, teaching for doctrines the commandments of men."
>
> Matthew 15:8,9

This is also found in Mark 10:18,19.

The question was raised in Matthew 19:16, "Good Master, what good thing shall I do that I may have eternal life?" In verse 17 Jesus answered, "Keep the *commandments*."

> "Woe unto you, scribes and Pharisees, hypocrites! for ye pay tithe of mint and anise and cummin, and have omitted the weightier matters of the law, judgment, mercy, and faith: these ought ye to have done, and not to leave the other undone."
>
> Matthew 23:23

I think I can guess what you may be thinking about now. The *Ten Commandments* were tough enough, but when Jesus said to place God above all else and love your neighbor as yourself, you, like me, may have considered giving up. Can I keep God's *commandments*? Then I discovered a Scripture that told me what sin is, a definition I could work

God's Will

with, one that gave me understanding and reason.

> "Whosoever committeth sin transgresseth also the law: for sin is the transgression of the law."
>
> 1 John 3:4

You cannot fight sin if you cannot define it, so it is good for us to place this definition in our minds. Memorize it, so that you can recall it any time.

As we progress through this section on the *commandments* you should be picking up on the point that the *Ten Commandments* of the Old Testament, and the statement Jesus made in the New Testament, all speak the same message.

> "And Jesus answered him, The first of all the *commandments* is, Hear, O Israel; The Lord our God is one Lord: And thou shalt love the Lord thy God with all thy heart, and with all thy soul, and with all thy mind, and with all thy strength: this is the first *commandment*. And the second is like, namely this, Thou shalt love thy neighbor as thyself. There is none other *commandment* greater than these."
>
> Mark 12:29-31

The greatest *commandments* are to place God first and love your neighbor as yourself. This certainly was not new, but it was to these people. The *Ten Commandments* have always taught this. Check this out for yourself. The first three *commandments* teach us how to love God. The fourth *commandment* is speaking a little of both: It is telling us to take one day to rest, both for ourselves and those we employ (love for our neighbor). Also that we should remember on this day where all our blessings come from and give thanks

The Will of God Part One

and keep the day holy. This is showing our love for God. Does this not teach love for God and our neighbor?

The fifth through the tenth *commandments* teach us how to love our neighbor as ourselves. Mark 12:3 tells us to love your neighbor as yourself. How do you do this? Let's stop here and read Exodus 20:12-17.

Loving my mother and father certainly was not tough for me to do (verse 12). I think this is a livable request of love. My parents always honored God and gave me the same choice. But remember this, our best source of moral guidance comes only from God.

I know that if I take someone's life, there will be retaliation, either by the law or someone else (verse 13). I can live with this request.

Adultery would bring heartbreak to my wife, children, the church, and bring discredit to my reputation. I can live without hurting my family, my friends, and God.

I know that stealing will also bring retaliation (verse 15). This is not a way of showing love.

If I tell something false about my neighbor, do you think he or she would love me for it (verse 16)? Of course not!

It is a joy to see my neighbor happy and prosperous, and I will not allow myself to lust after the things my neighbor has, for if I should desire to take from my neighbor it would only bring hurt to him (verse 17).

Honesty is the balance that will meter justice to all.
To deceive is folly that will return only to haunt.

Luke tells us about a certain lawyer who questioned, "Master, what shall I do to inherit eternal life?" (Luke 10:25).

Jesus responded with a question: "What is written in the law? how readest thou?" (Luke 10:26).

Then the lawyer replied, "Thou shalt love the Lord thy

God's Will

God with all thy heart, and with all thy soul, and with all thy strength, and with all thy mind; and thy neighbor as thyself" (verse 27). Jesus told him to do this and "thou shalt live" (verse 28).

The lawyer quoted the *Ten Commandments*. Do you agree? It would be hard not to agree after all we have read thus far.

In John 5:42 Jesus is telling the people that they do not have the love of God in them. "*I am* come in my Father's name [God] and ye receive me not" (verse 43). "Do not think that I will accuse you to the Father" (verse 45). "Moses . . . wrote of me, [speaking of the *Ten Commandments*, as well as I 'AM that I AM] But if ye believed not his writings, how shall ye believe my words?" (verses 46,47).

Jesus said that His doctrine is from God (John 7:16). "If any man will do his *will*, he shall know of the doctrine, whether it be of God or whether I speak of myself" (verse 17). In verse 19 Jesus said, Moses gave you the *law*, yet you are not keeping the *law*. "Why go ye about to kill me?"

Jesus said, "A new *commandment* I give unto you, that ye love one another; as I have loved you" (John 13:34). Again, it is not really new, but new understanding for them, as well as for us today. In verse 35 Jesus said, "By this shall all men know that ye are my disciples, if ye have love one to another."

"If ye love me, keep my commandments."
John 14:15

Keep the *commandments* and you will be loved by the Father (God) and Jesus will know you. Love Him and He will love you and will show himself to you (John 14:21). If you love Jesus, you will keep His words (verse 23). If you don't love Him, you will not keep His sayings. The words Jesus spoke are the words of the Father who sent Him (verse 24).

The Will of God Part One

If you keep His words, you may ask what you will and it shall be done for you (John 15:7). If you keep His *commandments*, you shall abide in His love (verse 10).

When you pray for your friend, do not pray for what *you* think is best for your friend, but pray for what *is* best in God's sight and it will be best for your friend. Do not try to push yourself ahead of God as far as wisdom and understanding are concerned. Healing is part of the *Will of God*, one of the nine gifts of the Spirit (1 Corinthians 12:9), but only if it is best for everyone concerned. Remember to keep your prayers in order: Love God and place Him first, ahead of everyone and everything else, then remember to love your neighbor as yourself. God knows what is best.

Do you recall the lady I wrote about (chapter 4) who was blaming God for the death of her child? Placing God first in our lives is really hard to do sometimes, but it must happen if we want His love in our own lives. The lady was placing her child ahead of God, possibly without ever recognizing this fact. She was the one who did not know Love well enough to grant "Love" first place in her life. God is Love, and Love is for mankind; consequently, she thought her prayers were rising no higher than the ceiling.

God has an overview of all our lives. He knows what is best for you and yours. A "no" from God may be best and a more merciful answer. This child is with God in paradise. If the child had lived he may have died later on, in the depths of sin, with its eternal punishment. Always allow God to have first place, and be able to give thanks even when the answer is no.

> "If ye keep my commandments, ye shall abide in my love; even as I have kept my Father's commandments, and abide in his love, These things have I spoken unto you, that my joy might remain in you, and that your joy might be full. This is my

God's Will

commandment, That ye love one another, as I have loved you. Greater love hath no man than this, that a man lay down his life for his friends. Ye are my friends, if ye do whatsoever I command you . . . These things I command you, that ye love one another . . . If I had not come and spoken unto them, they had not had sin: but now they have no cloak for their sin."
John 15:10-14,17,22

If it were not for the *commandments,* we would not know what sin is. "Whosoever committeth sin transgresseth also the *law*" (1 John 3:4).

"For the wrath of God is revealed from heaven against all ungodliness and unrighteousness of men, who hold the truth in unrighteousness."
Romans 1:18

Paul writes in Romans 1:20-22 that they (all of us) are without excuse, they knew God, they professed to be wise, but became as fools.

"Wherefore God also gave them up to uncleanness through the lusts of their own hearts, to dishonor their own bodies between themselves."
Romans 1:24

They changed the truth of God into a lie and worshiped and served the creature more than the Creator (verse 25).

"For this cause God gave them up unto vile affections: for even their women did change the natural use into that which is against nature: And likewise also the men, leaving the natural use of the

The Will of God Part One

woman, burned in their lust one toward another; men with men working that which is unseemly, and receiving in themselves that recompence of their error which was meet. And even as they did not like to retain God in their knowledge, God gave them over to a reprobate mind, to do those things which are not convenient; Being filled with all unrighteousness, fornication, wickedness, covetousness, maliciousness; full of envy, murder, debate, deceit, malignity; whisperers, Backbiters, haters of God, despiteful, proud, boasters, inventors of evil things, disobedient to parents, Without understanding, covenantbreakers, without natural affection, implacable, unmerciful: Who, knowing the judgment of God, that they which commit such things are worthy of death, not only do the same, but have pleasure in them that do them."
Romans 1:26-32

God, because He is Love, has given mankind a choice. You can live or die by your own choice. Which do you prefer—eternal life in paradise, or eternal damnation, which is hell and the lake of fire? You have only a few short years at the most to make your choice.

"Therefore thou art inexcusable, O man . . . The judgment of God is according to truth against them, which commit such things . . . There is no respect of persons with God. For as many as have sinned without *law* shall also perish without *law*: and as many as have sinned in the *law* shall be judged by the *law* . . . the doers of the *law* shall be justified."
Romans 2:1,2,11,12,13

God's Will

"That the righteousness of the law might be fulfilled in us, who walk not after the flesh, but after the Spirit."
Romans 8:4

"Love worketh no ill to his neighbor: therefore love is the fulfilling of the law."
Romans 13:10

Keeping the *law* or *commandments* is love fulfilled.

"Use not liberty for an occasion to the flesh, but by love serve one another. For all the *law* is fulfilled in one word, even in this; *Thou shalt love thy neighbor as thyself*" (Galatians 5:13,14). Verses 19-21 describe the works of the flesh. Verse 21 says, "They which do such things shall *not* inherit the kingdom of God." The works of the flesh are adultery, fornication, uncleanness, lasciviousness, idolatry, witchcraft, hatred, variance, emulations, wrath, strife, seditions, heresies, envyings, murders, drunkenness, reveling, and such like (verses 19-21).

Galatians 5:22-26 describes the life of the Spirit-filled person. What can you expect to see produced in a Spirit-filled life? "But the fruit of the Spirit is love, joy, peace, long-suffering, gentleness, goodness, faith, Meekness, temperance: against such there is no law" (verses 22,23). Which sounds best to you, the works of the flesh or the fruit of the Spirit? Choose wisely.

"If we live in the Spirit, let us also walk in the Spirit."
Galatians 5:25

Why not? It sounds good to me!

"And whatsoever you do in word or deed, do all in

the name of the Lord Jesus, giving thanks to God and the Father by him."
Colossians 3:17

Colossians 3:18-24 gives advice to wives and husbands, children and servants. "He that does wrong shall receive for the wrong he has done: and there is no respect of persons" (verse 25).

If you don't love as you have read in these Scriptures, your disobedience will come back on you like a bad storm and you will not receive the reward of the inheritance.

"Knowing this, that the law is not made for a righteous man, but for the lawless and disobedient, for the ungodly and for sinners, for unholy and profane, for murderers of fathers and murderers of mothers, for manslayers, For whoremongers, for them that defile themselves with mankind, for menstealers, for liars, for perjured persons, and if there be any other thing that is contrary to sound doctrine."
1 Timothy 1:9,10

"And being made perfect, he became the author of eternal salvation unto all them that obey him."
Hebrews 5:9

"And hereby we do know that we know him, if we keep his commandments. He that saith, I know him, and keepeth not his *commandments*, is a liar, and the truth is not in him."
1 John 2:3,4

If we keep His *commandments* (His Word) the love of God is perfected in us: hereby we know that we are in Him (verse 5). John continued: "Brethren, I write no new *commandment* unto you, but an old *commandment* ye had from the beginning" (verse 7). If you love your brother, you abide in light. If not, you are in darkness (verse 9).

> "He that loveth his brother abideth in the light, and there is none occasion of stumbling in him . . . And the world passeth away, and the lust thereof: but he that doeth the will of God abideth forever."
> 1 John 2:10,17

> "And now little children, abide in him; that, when he shall appear, we may have confidence, and not be ashamed before him at his coming. If ye know that he is *righteous,* ye know that everyone that doeth *righteousness* is born of him."
> 1 John 2:28,29

John wrote, "*Sin is the transgression of the law*" (1 John 3:4). "Whosoever abideth in him [God] sinneth not" (verse 6). "Let no man deceive you: he that doeth righteousness is righteous, even as he [Christ] is righteous" (verse 7).

> "Whosoever is born of God doth not commit sin . . . For this is the message that ye heard from the beginning [speaking of the *Ten Commandments*], that we should love one another . . . He that loveth not his brother abideth in death."
> 1 John 3:9,11,14

> "And whatsoever we ask, we receive of him, because we keep his *commandments*, and do those things that are pleasing in his sight."
> 1 John 3:22

The Will of God Part One

If you want your prayers answered, do the things that are pleasing in His sight.

Believe on the name of Jesus Christ and love one another as He commanded us to do (1 John 3:23). "He abideth in us, by the Spirit which he hath given us" (1 John 3:24).

> "Greater is he that is in you, than he that is in the world."
>
> 1 John 4:4

> "Beloved, let us love one another: for love is of God; and every one that loveth is born of God, and knoweth God."
>
> 1 John 4:7

"If we love one another, God dwelleth in us, and his love is perfected in us" (1 John 4:12). We know this because He has given us His Spirit (verse 13). "God is love; and he that dwelleth in love dwelleth in God, and God in him" (1 John 4:16).

> "And this commandment have we from him, That he who loveth God love his brother also."
>
> 1 John 4:21

If we keep the *commandments,* we love God and love the children of God (1 John 5:2). "For this is the love of God, that we keep his *commandments"* (verse 3). Whoever is born of God *overcomes* the world (verse 4).

> "Who is he that overcometh the world, but he that believeth that Jesus is the Son of God?"
>
> 1 John 5:5

We should love one another (2 John 1:5). You have

God's Will

heard it from the beginning. "This is love, that we walk after his *commandments*" (verse 6). "Whosoever transgresseth, and abideth not in the doctrine of Christ, hath not God" (verse 9). If you abide in the doctrine of Christ, you abide in both the Father and the Son.

> "And he that overcometh, and keepeth my works unto the end, to him will I give power over the nations."
> Revelation 2:26

> "Blessed are they that do his commandments, that they may have right to the tree of life, and may enter in through the gates into the city."
> Revelation 22:14

The *Ten Commandments* may seem a lot newer to you now. God loves you so much He wants you to have the abundant life, both here and now, this very moment, and throughout eternity. Read the Ten Commandments again in Exodus 20:1-17.

God knows that true love is not sin. As we have said before, God is love. Sin is the opposite of love. In order to fully understand love, we need to fully understand God. The *Ten Commandments* teach us how to love. Love is not without a disciplined life. After reading the preceding Scriptures, ask yourself this question: *Can I love my neighbor in light of these Scriptures?* Your answer will have to be yes. If not, you do not yet understand what love is.

The world's definition of love as found in your dictionary is much different than what God teaches in His Word. Check your dictionary. That's right, stop here and check the definition: "Love: Strong passionate affection for a person of the opposite sex." The complete definition is quite lengthy, but the point is that you know the difference between the world's definition and the definition of love, God's way. Some of the larger dictionaries may give only a short definition of God's love, so it is very important to know the true Love.

Joshua 1:8,9 is a good way to end this chapter.

> "This book of the law shall not depart out of thy mouth; but thou shalt meditate therein day and night, that thou mayest observe to do according to all that is written therein: for then thou shalt make thy way prosperous, and then thou shalt have good success. Have not I commanded thee? Be strong and of a good courage; be not afraid, neither be thou dismayed: for the Lord thy God is with thee whithersoever thou goest."
>
> Joshua 1:8,9

This concludes our study of "Part One" of *The Will of God*. I hope your mind has been awakened to a new and more complete understanding of the wonderful *Ten Commandments*.

Chapter 5

Summary

The Ten Commandments are given to mankind as a guide to a happy, prosperous, healthy, and successful life.

To be happy is to receive the *commandments*, and do them. Being prosperous is to understand the spiritual value of the *Ten Commandments*. Being healthy is the life given to us by doing the *commandments*. To be successful is to understand God's love given through the *commandments*.

How to love God and your neighbor is made very clear in the wonderful *Ten Commandments*.

CHAPTER 6

THE WILL OF GOD PART TWO

Since the dawn of creation I have watched you make mistakes, and I have watched you cry bitterly because of the results of sin. So dear friend, I sent My Son, Jesus, to shed His blood that you could better know how I feel for you. Jesus dwelt among you in the form of flesh like yourself. He was tempted just like you are tempted. Therefore, He knows how to help you and judge mankind. He died that you need never sacrifice an animal for the forgiveness of sin. Now He sits here beside Me and tells Me your cares both good and bad. He also tells Me about the things you are thankful for. My Son, Jesus, will hear your prayers if you are sincere. Jesus is part of My Will for you—that you might have life more abundantly. Please accept Him as your friend. You could not possibly have a better friend, for it is through Him we shall meet someday.

JESUS CHRIST—SON OF GOD
GOD THE SON
MEDIATOR OF THE WILL OF GOD

This entire book is about Jesus and all that He brought to mankind from the Father God.

As I researched the Word of God regarding the Will of God, many wonderful things were revealed to me about Jesus:

1. Jesus is the God of the Old Testament.
2. Jesus is the Creator of the heavens and the earth.
3. Jesus wrote the Ten Commandments.
4. Jesus is the great "I AM" of the Old Testament.
5. Before Abraham was "I AM."
6. Jesus presented to Abraham and his descendents the *Old Testament* (Will).
7. Jesus presented to all mankind the *New Testament* (Will).
8. It was necessary that Jesus come to earth and die since He was the testator of both Wills.
9. The Ten Commandments are still a very important part of the *New Will*.
10. Jesus sent the Holy Spirit to man, from the Father God.
11. The *New Will* includes all mankind, every race, tribe, and nation, bond or free, man or woman, married or single.
12. Jesus brought everlasting life, given through both the *Old* and *New Wills*.
13. Jesus agreed with the Father God and allowed His own death to take place in order to validate both W*ills*.
14. Jesus was the last death (blood sacrifice) for the forgiveness of sins. The blood of animals cannot take

away our sins.
15. Animal sacrifice made in the *Old Testament* was a symbol of the blood sacrifice Jesus gave to make valid both *Old* and *New Wills*. Jesus is God and could not die until He became human.
16. Jesus has risen from the grave and is now sitting at the right hand of God the Father and intercedes to the Father on our behalf.

Without Jesus there would be no *Will*, *Old* or *New*. Because of Jesus we can:

- Be a recipient of the *Will*.
- Be a son or daughter of God, because of the *Will*.
- Know the Father God (if you know Jesus, you know the Father, for they are one).
- Know the Holy Spirit.
- Be a joint heir with Jesus.
- Talk to the Father God.
- Talk to God the Son.
- Talk to the Holy Spirit, and have the Holy Spirit intercede for us when we don't know how we should pray.
- Know that the love of God can be perfected in us.
- Know for sure that we can inherit eternal life.

Yes, because of Jesus we can all have the same benefits. Words fail me when I attempt to express how I feel about Jesus and all He has done for me. My life has changed so completely since Jesus has taken full control, that the adjectives describing the change are hard to pen.

Life in this world has its "ups and downs," tragedies, sorrows, happy times, and hardships, but if we have Jesus as our friend and Savior the happy times are happier and the down times are bearable, and in the end we inherit an eternal home where there are no more problems, trials, sickness,

God's Will

pain, nor death.

Let me tell you a true story about a wild pumpkin that suddenly began growing in our backyard during a drought. To me, it's a story about life on earth, and that God will be with you through the dry seasons, and on into eternal life.

The Will of God Part Two

The Wild Pumpkin

The land was dry, and so was the grass. So dry in fact that it would crunch underfoot as we walked across the lawn. Drought was talked about all over the nation.

One day to my surprise, a wild pumpkin sprouted in the backyard of our home. It had survived only because we did not need to cut the grass since the grass was too dry to grow. If it had not been for this fact, the pumpkin would have been cut off by the lawn mower and we would not have known it had ever been there. The vine grew and grew until it had reached out 15 feet from its starting place. Then the rains began to fall again, the drought was over, but the vine was firmly in place, continuing to grow until it finally reached approximately 32 feet in length.

Every morning the lovely vine brought forth blossoms that measured 4 or 5 inches across, having a perfect star-shaped, yellowish-orange beauty that seemed to scream, "Look! Look at me, and listen! If it were not for the drought, I would not be here."

We had other flowers in the yard that we were watering and carefully looking after, trying to keep them alive. They were nice, but there was something special about this vine, something very different. So different was this vine, I simply had to write about it. The probability of this happening in such dry weather is awesome. Then on top of this, where did the seed come from? We for sure did not plant it. Nevertheless, every morning I was blessed and impressed by the beauty and brightness of two to four blossoms. I estimate there must have been thirty or more, but only one blossom made a pumpkin. The rest lived only a short while, dried up, and eventually dropped from the vine. The one pumpkin grew to maturity, even turning orange. It was a beautiful specimen. I thought to myself, *There must be a hundred seeds or more by which this pumpkin can reproduce itself.*

God's Will

One day, to our complete surprise and amazement, this vine produced another pumpkin that grew and grew until it had surpassed the first pumpkin in growth and became the more beautiful of the two. The vine that seemed to be a one-pumpkin vine became a two-pumpkin vine even after it had matured. It found new strength after the rains came, put down new roots, and continued to grow.

There are, in retrospect, a number of things that God may be telling you and me through this story. Time has passed since I first wrote about "The Wild Pumpkin." Maturity has reached this life of mine. Maybe the Lord was telling me back then that a drought was coming to my life in which it may appear that everything I worked for was in vain. Do you suppose God was telling me that when maturity comes and income goes, He will still be with me, new roots are now growing, and the new, more beautiful pumpkin is about to begin its growth. Speaking for myself now, after retirement, I am anxious to see this new development in my life.

Maybe you would enjoy using "The Wild Pumpkin" story as a way of looking forward or for thinking back through your life:

1. Picture yourself as the wild pumpkin seed that germinated and you became the vine.
2. The ideas and plans you have made or will be making may represent the blossoms.
3. The dry weather may represent a job loss or a failure in life.
4. The mature pumpkin may represent your first successful venture in life.
5. The new roots and new rains may represent a new strength and greater promises.
6. The internal seeds may represent ideas and concepts that will germinate after your life has passed and will

The Will of God Part Two

live on and generate more seed.
7. The second most beautiful and larger pumpkin may represent your second opportunity after maturity which may be your retirement, your aspirations, or your eternal hopes.

I sincerely hope this true story of "The Wild Pumpkin" stirred your mind and quickened your step as it did mine. We have no need to be discouraged or think for one moment that God would ever turn His back on the one He died for. That one is you.

It may be that you already know *the Will of God*, you have accepted it, and now your life is reflecting His beauty in different facets of your daily living as depicted in "The Wild Pumpkin" story. It may be, because of the wonderful *Will of God*, that you now allow the love of God to reach out from you and cause another wild pumpkin to grow and beautify the drought-stricken land around you.

Because of Jesus, this wild pumpkin seed, Bill Childers by name, is trying to do what he can to help someone else see that he or she can bring beauty and light to a world that is crying for help.

My love for Jesus and all that He has brought to all mankind is almost overwhelming. My cup runs over with joy, thanksgiving, and peace of mind.

Knowing the total *Will of God* came late in my life, but it did come to me. The blessings of knowing it will live on eternally. Don't be discouraged when life hands you a "let down." Look up to Jesus, don't be afraid to ask for help, because He really does want you to ask. Jesus can be your dearest friend.

It is wonderful to know that Jesus is sitting at the right hand of God the Father, waiting to hear from you. Talk to Him. He wants to hear from you today.

Chapter 6

Summary

Jesus looked down from heaven and saw mankind weeping over the effects of sin. Because of His love, He gave up paradise and brought the Father's *Will* to man. Jesus, the mediator and testator, is offering to all mankind this wonderful *Will*. Yes, it is for all who will accept and do it. Will you receive it? We could not possibly receive a more rewarding *Will* than this.

CHAPTER 7

THE WILL OF GOD
PART THREE

I can see your weakness and inability to cope with sin and the problems of your world. Through Jesus I sent the Holy Spirit into this world of yours that you might have strength to overcome sin and the wisdom you need to understand the things of this Will. I will to you the gift of the Holy Spirit. There are nine gifts of the Spirit which you may seek. They are part of My Will for you, but of all the gifts I promised, place love at the top. Love for your Creator and love for your neighbor.

God's Will

GIFT OF THE HOLY SPIRIT THROUGH THE WILL OF GOD

I will never forget when I first heard about the Holy Spirit. I thought it was the most wonderful news I had ever heard. Wow! Strength and power to overcome sin. I always wanted to do right, but it was always a big struggle. When I wanted to do good, evil was always present. It seemed all was in vain, and there was just no use trying. Then I heard about the Holy Spirit, and He came to me when I sought Him through Jesus Christ. My life has not been the same since that day. You too can have this new insight on the subject. You may already have received His infilling, but if you have not, feast your eyes on the good news. It is for you through the *New Will of God*.

HOLY GHOST

The Spirit of God; third person of the trinity; Holy Spirit.[1]

COMFORTER

"If ye love me, keep my commandments. And I will pray the Father, and he shall give you another Comforter, that he may abide with you for ever; Even the Spirit of truth; whom the world cannot receive, because it seeth him not, neither knoweth him: but ye know him; for he dwelleth with you, and shall be in you. I will not leave you comfortless: I will come to you . . . But the Comforter, which is the Holy Ghost, whom the Father will send in my name, he shall teach you all things,

and bring all things to your remembrance, whatsoever I have said unto you."
John 14:15-18,26

The Comforter and the Holy Ghost are one and the same.

GRACE

As related to the last *Will of God* and the Holy Spirit, grace is mentioned 38 times in the Old Testament and 127 times in the New Testament.

Grace: Unmerited divine assistance given man for his regeneration or sanctification; a state of sanctification enjoyed through divine grace; a virtue coming from God.[2]

Grace: God's free and undeserved favor to, and love for mankind; influence of God operating in man to improve or strengthen: "But where sin abounded, grace did much more abound" (Romans 5:20); the condition of being influenced and favored by God. Grace, in a sense, is that which conforms us to God, the Creator; mercy; clemency; pardon; forgiveness.[1]

BLESSED

Blessed: Holy; sacred; the blessed Trinity; enjoying the favor of heaven; fortunate: "Blessed are the pure in heart: for they shall see God" (Matthew 5:8).

SANCTIFICATION

Sanctification: The act of sanctifying or making holy: "God hath from the beginning chosen you to salvation through sanctification of the Spirit and belief of the truth" (2 Thessalonians 2:13); the state of being sanctified; purification from sin;

consecration.[1]

"For this is the will of God, even your sanctification, that ye should abstain from fornication."
                                                1 Thessalonians 4:3

SANCTIFIED

Sanctified: Made holy; set apart for sacred services; consecrated; sacred.[1]

The following Scriptures will reveal light on the great and wonderful gift from God the Father, through Jesus Christ, which is the third person of the Holy Trinity: The Holy Ghost.

John the Baptist proclaimed, "I indeed baptize you with water unto repentance: but he that cometh after me . . . shall baptize you with the *Holy Ghost,* and with fire" (Matthew 3:11). See also Mark 1:8, Luke 3:16, John 1:33, Acts 1:5, and Acts 11:16.

"All power is given unto me in heaven and in earth. Go ye therefore, and teach all nations, baptizing them in the name of the Father, and of the Son, and of the *Holy Ghost:* Teaching them to observe all things whatsoever I have commanded you: and, lo, I am with you always, even unto the end of the world. Amen."
                                                Matthew 28:18-20

How do you feel about these words: *Holy Ghost, Holy Spirit, Comforter, Grace, Blessed, Sanctification,* and *Sanctified?*

I remember very well the first time I heard the word

sanctification. It really excited me, but I wondered about it. *Is it really true?* I began to search the Word of God and asked others who knew this work of *grace* and had experienced *sanctification.*

Light began to dawn upon me. Jesus sent the *Comforter* and I received Him, filling my life with new spiritual strength that I had never known before. What a privilege to know, understand, and receive the *Holy Spirit* into my life.

If you are not comfortable with these words, it may be because you don't understand, just as I didn't understand. The things people do not understand, they fear. The thing I hope to accomplish in this section is to bring understanding regarding these wonderful words so that the new light will chase away the fear.

> "For this is the *will of God*, even your *sanctification*, that ye should abstain from fornication."
> 1 Thessalonians 4:3

Yes, *sanctification* is part of the *Will of God.* Praise the name of Jesus for this gift. This is your gift also, if you will ask Jesus and accept the total *Will.*

John baptized with water, but He, meaning Jesus, "shall baptize you with the *Holy Ghost"* (Mark 1:4,8).

All sins, including blasphemies, shall be forgiven, except "blaspheme against the *Holy Ghost* hath never forgiveness, but is in danger of eternal damnation" (Mark 3:28,29). Be very careful, my friend. Do not insult, condemn, belittle, or speak irreverently of the *Holy Ghost.* Do not condemn or you may be condemning yourself.

"Whosoever speaketh against the *Holy Ghost*, it shall not be forgiven him, neither in this world, neither in the world to come" (Matthew 12:32). See also Luke 12:10.

Luke 2 is the beginning of New Testament *grace.*

The Will of God Part Three

"And the child [Jesus] grew and became strong in *spirit*, filled with wisdom; and the *grace* of God was upon him."
Luke 2:40

If you desire to receive the *Holy Spirit*, ask Jesus. He is very willing to give you the *Holy Spirit*. As I have said before, this is part of the *Will of God*.

"Ask, and it shall be given you; seek, and ye shall find; knock, and it shall be opened unto you . . . If ye then, being evil, know how to give good gifts unto your children; how much more shall your heavenly Father give the *Holy Spirit* to them that ask him?"
Luke 11:9,13

"And John bare record, saying, I saw the *Spirit* descending from heaven like a dove, and it abode upon him [Jesus]. And I knew him not: but he that sent me to baptize with water, the same said unto me, Upon whom thou shalt see the *Spirit* descending, and remaining on him, the same is he which baptizeth with the *Holy Ghost*. And I saw, and bare record that this is the Son of God."
John 1:32-34

"And the Word [Jesus] was made flesh and dwelt among us, (and we beheld his glory, the glory as of the only begotten [Son] of the Father,) full of *grace* and truth."
John 1:14

God's Will

Jesus said, "Except a man be born of water and of the *Spirit*, he cannot enter the kingdom of God. That which is born of the flesh is flesh; and that which is born of the *Spirit* is *spirit*."

John 3:5,6

"But whosoever drinketh of the water that I [Jesus] shall give him shall never thirst; but the water that I shall give him shall be in him a well of water springing up into everlasting life."

John 4:14

Jesus is referring to the baptism of the *Holy Ghost*.

"It is the *Spirit* that quickeneth [makes alive]; the flesh profiteth [helps] nothing: the words that I [Jesus] speak unto you, they are *spirit,* and they are life."

John 6:63

"In the last day, that great day of the feast, Jesus stood and cried, saying, If any man thirst, let him come unto me, and drink. He that believeth on me, as the scripture hath said, out of his belly shall flow rivers of living water. (But this spake he of the Spirit, which they that believe on him should receive: for the Holy Ghost was not yet given; because that Jesus was not yet glorified.)"

John 7:37-39

"Then said Jesus to those Jews which believed on him, If ye continue in my word, then are ye my disciples indeed; And ye shall know the truth, and the truth shall make you free."

John 8:31,32

The Will of God Part Three

"This is he that came by water and blood, even Jesus Christ; not by water only, but by water and blood. And it is the Spirit that beareth witness, because the *Spirit is truth.*"
1 John 5:6

"But when the *Comforter* is come, whom I will send unto you from the Father, even the *Spirit* of *truth*, which proceedeth from the Father, he shall testify of me [Jesus]."
John 15:26

"Nevertheless I tell you the *truth*; it is expedient for you that I [Jesus] go away: for if I go not away, the *Comforter* will not come unto you; but if I depart, I will send him unto you."
John 16:7

"Howbeit when he, the *Spirit of truth,* is come, he will guide you into all *truth*: for he shall not speak of himself; but whatsoever he shall hear, that shall he speak: and he will show you things to come."
John 16:13

"I [Jesus] *sanctify* myself, that they also might be *sanctified* through the *truth.*"
John 17:19

John 20 tells about the disciples receiving the *Holy Ghost.*

"Then said Jesus to them again, Peace be unto you: as my Father hath sent me, even so send I you. And when he had said this, he breathed on them, and saith unto them, Receive ye the Holy Ghost."

John 20:21,22

"John truly baptized with water; but ye shall be baptized with the *Holy Ghost*" (Acts 1:5). Do you need more strength to overcome the evil one?

"But ye shall receive power after that the *Holy Ghost* is come upon you: and ye shall be witnesses unto me both in Jerusalem, and in all Judea, and in Samaria, and unto the uttermost part of the earth."

Acts 1:8

"And when the day of Pentecost was fully come, they were all with one accord in one place . . . And they were all filled with the Holy Ghost, and began to speak with other tongues, as the Spirit gave them utterance."

Acts 2:1,4

"Then Peter said unto them, Repent, and be baptized every one of you in the name of Jesus Christ for the remission of sins, and ye shall receive the gift of the Holy Ghost. For the promise is unto you, and to your children, and to all that are afar off, even as many as the Lord our God shall call."

Acts 2:38,39

"When they had prayed . . . they were all filled with the *Holy Ghost*" (Acts 4:31). They had boldness after they were filled. They were of one heart and one soul. They had all things common.

"And with great power gave the apostles witness

of the resurrection of the Lord Jesus: and great *grace* was upon them all."

Acts 4:33

"We ought to obey God rather than men" (Acts 5:29). Verses 30 and 31 say the people slew Jesus and hung Him on a tree, but the Prince God was sent to be our Savior, to give repentance to Israel and forgiveness of sins. "We are his witnesses of these things; and so is also the *Holy Ghost,* whom God hath given to them that obey him" (Acts 5:32).

When the apostles heard that Samaria had received the Word of God, Peter and John were sent to pray for them that they might receive the *Holy Ghost.* So far none of the Samaritans had received the *Holy Ghost.* They laid their hands on them, and they received the *Holy Ghost* (Acts 8:14-17).

Ananias, by Jesus' request, went to Paul in his blindness that he, Paul, might receive his sight (healing) and be filled with the *Holy Ghost* (Acts 9:17).

> "And immediately there fell from his eyes as it had been scales: and he received his sight forthwith, and arose, and was baptized."
>
> Acts 9:18

As Peter spoke, the *Holy Ghost* fell on all of them which heard the Word. The Gentiles also received the *Holy Ghost.* They heard them speak with tongues and magnify God (Acts 10:44-46).

> "Can any man forbid water, that these should not be baptized, which have received the *Holy Ghost* as well as we? And he commanded them to be baptized in the name of the Lord."
>
> Acts 10:47,48

God's Will

In Acts 11, Peter tells the Jewish Christians that the Gentiles had received the *Holy Ghost*.

> "And as I began to speak, the Holy Ghost fell on them, as on us at the beginning. Then remembered I the word of the Lord, how that he said, John indeed baptized with water; but ye shall be baptized with the Holy Ghost. For as much then as God gave them the like gift as he did unto us, who believed on the Lord Jesus Christ, what was I, that I could withstand God? When they heard these things, they held their peace, and glorified God, saying, Then hath God also to the Gentiles granted repentance unto life."
>
> Acts 11:15-18

When Barnabas arrived in Antioch and saw the Gentiles had received the *grace* (a state of holiness enjoyed by the folk at Antioch) of God, he was glad and exhorted them all to cleave unto the Lord (Acts 11:23).

> "For he [Barnabas] was a good man, and full of the *Holy Ghost* and of faith: and much people was added unto the Lord."
>
> Acts 11:24

In Acts 13:43, Paul and Barnabas are asking the Jews and religious converts to continue in the *grace* of God.

At Iconium Paul and Barnabas spoke boldly for the Lord and "gave testimony unto the word of his *grace*, and [the Lord] granted signs and wonders to be done by their hands" (Acts 14:3).

Paul and Barnabas, "thence sailed to Antioch, from whence they had been recommended [committed] to the *grace* of God for the work which they fulfilled" (Acts

14:26).

In Acts 15, Peter is speaking to the Council of Jerusalem.

> "Men and brethren, ye know how that a good while ago God made choice among us, that the Gentiles by my mouth should hear the word of the gospel [good news], and believe. And God, which knoweth the hearts, bare them witness, giving them the *Holy Ghost,* even as he did unto us; And put no difference between us and them, purifying their hearts by faith . . . But we believe that through the *grace* of the Lord Jesus Christ we shall be saved, even as they."
>
> Acts 15:7-9,11

The question was asked by Paul of certain disciples at Ephesus, "Have ye received the *Holy Ghost* since ye believed [that Jesus is the Son of God]?" (Acts 19:1,2). The answer came back that they had not even heard that there was a *Holy Ghost.* Paul then asked, "Unto what then were ye baptized? And they said, Unto John's baptism" (which is water baptism unto repentance). Paul said to the people, "John verily [truly] baptized with the baptism of repentance, saying unto the people, that they should believe on him which should come after him, that is, on Christ Jesus" (verse 4).

> "When they heard this, they were baptized in the name of the Lord Jesus. And when Paul had laid his hands upon them, the *Holy Ghost* came on them . . . And all of the men were about twelve."
>
> Acts 19:5-7

Paul addresses the Ephesian elders, saying:

God's Will

"And now, brethren, I commend you to God, and to the word of his *grace*, which is able to build you up, and to give you an inheritance among all them which are *sanctified*."

Acts 20:32

In Acts 26:14-17, Paul is telling King Agrippa of his conversion and of his call to tell the Gentiles about Jesus, repeating what Jesus told him to do.

"To open their eyes, and to turn them from darkness to light, and from the power of Satan unto God, that they may receive forgiveness of sins, and inheritance among them which are *sanctified* by faith that is in me [Jesus]."

Acts 26:18

Paul, speaking to the Romans about Jesus Christ, said:

"By whom we have received grace and apostleship, for obedience to the faith among all nations, for his name: Among whom are ye also the called of Jesus Christ: To all that be in Rome, beloved of God, called to be saints: *Grace* to you and peace from God our Father, and the Lord Jesus Christ."

Romans 1:5-7

"Being justified freely by his *grace* through the redemption that is in Christ Jesus."

Romans 3:24

"Now to him that worketh [or lives by the law of circumcision for his wages] is the reward not reckoned [given] of *grace,* but of debt . . . for where no law is, there is no transgression. Therefore it is of faith, that it might be by *grace* [to receive *grace* is by faith]."

Romans 4:4,15,16

"Being justified by faith, we have peace with God through our Lord Jesus Christ" (Romans 5:1). Through Jesus Christ, "we have access by faith into this *grace* wherein we stand, and rejoice in hope of the glory of God" (verse 2). We glory in tribulations also, for it brings patience (verse 3).

"And patience, experience; and experience hope: And hope maketh not ashamed; because the love of God is shed abroad in our hearts by the *Holy Ghost* which is given to us. For when we were yet without *strength*, in due time Christ died for the ungodly."

Romans 5:4-6

"The *grace* of God, and the gift by *grace*, which is by one man, Jesus Christ, hath abounded unto many."

Romans 5:15

"For if by one man's offense [Adam's sin] death reigned by one [Adam]; much more they which receive abundance of *grace* and of the gift of righteousness shall reign in life by one, Jesus Christ."

Romans 5:17

"But where sin abounded, *grace* did much more abound: That as sin hath reigned unto death, even so might *grace* reign through righteousness unto eternal life by Jesus Christ our Lord."

Romans 5:20,21

Remember, Jesus came to baptize with the *Holy Ghost*.

"What shall we say then? Shall we continue in sin, that *grace* may abound? God forbid. How shall we, that are dead to sin, live any longer therein? For sin shall not have dominion over you: for ye are not under the law, but under *grace*. What then? Shall we sin, because we are not under the law, but under *grace*? God forbid. But God be thanked, that ye were the servants of sin, but ye have obeyed from the heart that form of doctrine which has delivered you. Being then made free from sin, ye became servants of righteousness . . . so now yield your members servants to righteousness unto *holiness [sanctification]*."
Romans 6:1,2,14,15,17-19

"For when ye were the servants of sin, ye were free from righteousness. But now being made free from sin, and become servants to God, ye have your fruit unto *holiness*, and the end everlasting life. For the wages of sin is death; but the gift of God is eternal life through Jesus Christ our Lord."
Romans 6:20,22,23

"There is therefore now no condemnation to them which are in Christ Jesus, who walk not after the flesh, but after the Spirit. For the law of the Spirit of life in Christ Jesus hath made me free from the law of sin and death. For what the law could not do, in that it was weak through the flesh, God sending his own Son in the likeness of sinful flesh, and for sin, condemned sin in the flesh: That the righteousness of the law might be fulfilled in us, who walk not after the flesh, but after the Spirit.

The Will of God Part Three

For they that are after the flesh do mind the things of the flesh; but they that are after the Spirit, the things of the Spirit. For to be carnally minded is death: but to be spiritually minded is life and peace. Because the carnal mind is enmity against God: for it is not subject to the law of God, neither indeed can be."
Romans 8:1-7

"I beseech you therefore, brethren, by the mercies of God, that ye present your bodies a living sacrifice, *holy* . . . be ye transformed by the renewing of your mind, that ye may prove what is that good, and acceptable, and perfect *will of God*."
Romans 12:1,2

Paul, speaking of his ministry to the Gentiles, says, "Because of the *grace* that is given to me of God, that I should be the minister of Jesus Christ to the Gentiles, ministering the gospel of God, that the offering up of the Gentiles might be acceptable, being *sanctified* by the *Holy Ghost*"
(Romans 15:15,16).

"*Grace* be unto you, and peace, from God our Father, and from the Lord Jesus Christ. I thank my God always on your behalf, for the *grace* of God which is given you by Jesus Christ."
1 Corinthians 1:3,4

"Do you not know that the wicked will not inherit the kingdom of God? Do not be deceived."
1 Corinthians 6:9, NIV[4]

If you practice any of the following acts of sin, you will

God's Will

not enter the kingdom of God (1 Corinthians 6:9,10).[4]

> Sexually immoral: fornicators; sexual intercourse between unmarried persons.
>
> Idolaters
>
> Adulterers
>
> Male prostitutes
>
> Homosexual offenders
>
> Thieves
>
> The greedy
>
> Drunkards
>
> Slanderers
>
> Swindlers

Again I say: If you practice any of the above, do not expect to make it into eternal life.

> "And such were some of you: but ye are washed [repented and baptized] and *sanctified* [made holy—set apart], but ye are justified in the name of our Lord Jesus, and by the *Spirit* of our God."
> 1 Corinthians 6:11

The love of God gives you the choice of eternal life or eternal damnation. Which do you prefer? The choice is yours.

The Will of God Part Three

"What? know ye not that your body is the temple of the Holy Ghost which is in you, which ye have of God, and ye are not your own? For ye are bought with a price: therefore glorify God in your body, and in your spirit, which are God's."
1 Corinthians 6:19,20

Paul teaches concerning spiritual gifts in 1 Corinthians 12. He explains that no man can say Jesus is Lord, but by the *Holy Ghost*. There are different gifts, but the same *Spirit*. There are different *administrations*, but the same *Lord*. And there are different *operations*, "but it is the same *God* which worketh all in all" (verses 1-6).

"But the manifestation of the Spirit is given to every man to profit withal. For to one is given by the Spirit the word of wisdom; to another the word of knowledge by the same Spirit; To another faith by the same Spirit; to another the gifts of healing by the same Spirit; To another the working of miracles; to another prophecy; to another discerning of spirits; to another divers kinds of tongues; to another the interpretation of tongues: But all these worketh that one and the selfsame Spirit, dividing to every man severally as he will."
1 Corinthians 12:7-11

"But by the *grace* of God I am what I am: and his *grace* which was bestowed upon me was not in vain; but I labored more abundantly than they all: yet not I, but the *grace* of God which was with me."
1 Corinthians 15:10

"The *grace* of our Lord Jesus Christ be with you."
1 Corinthians 16:23

God's Will

"*Grace* be to you, and peace from God our Father, and from the Lord Jesus Christ."
2 Corinthians 1:2

Verses 3 and 4 speak of our Holy Father God, and our Lord Jesus Christ, and the God of all *comfort*; who is our *comfort* and strength in tribulation, "that we may be able to *comfort* them which are in any trouble, by the *comfort* wherewith we ourselves are *comforted* of God" (verse 4). *The Comforter* is the *Holy Ghost*.

Paul's summarizes his ministry in 2 Corinthians 6:1-10. He urges his fellow workers that they receive not the *grace* of God in vain, in all things approving ourselves as the ministers of God in any circumstance. How?

"By pureness, by knowledge, by longsuffering, by kindness, by the *Holy Ghost*, by love unfeigned [genuine love], By the word of *truth*, by the power of God, by the armor of righteousness on the right hand and the left."
2 Corinthians 6:6,7

"Having therefore these promises, dearly beloved, let us cleanse ourselves from all filthiness of the flesh and spirit, perfecting holiness in the fear of God."
2 Corinthians 7:1

Jesus spoke to Paul concerning Paul's thorn in the flesh:

"And he said unto me, My *grace* is sufficient for thee: for my strength is made perfect in weakness."
2 Corinthians 12:9

Paul's closing statement to the Corinthian church:

"The *grace* of the Lord Jesus Christ, and the love of God, and the communion [fellowship] of the *Holy Ghost*, be with you all. Amen."
2 Corinthians 13:14

Paul greets the church at Galatia in Galatians 1:3: "*Grace* be to you, and peace, from God the Father, and from our Lord Jesus Christ."

"Christ is become no effect unto you, whosoever of you are justified by the law [which is by circumcision, a token sign of the old covenant]; ye are fallen from *grace*. Walk in the *Spirit*, and ye shall not fulfill the lust of the flesh."
Galatians 5:4,16

The works of the flesh are evident (verses 19-21):

Adultery

Fornication

Uncleanness (impurity)

Lasciviousness (undisciplined—more to lust: lewd, lustful)

Idolatry

Witchcraft

Hatred

Variance

Emulations (jealousies)

Wrath

Strife

Seditions (divisions)

Heresies

Envying

Murders

Drunkenness

Revelings

> "They which do such things shall not inherit the kingdom of God."
>
> Galatians 5:21

How do you recognize a person who has received the *Holy Ghost* into his life? If he has flowing from his life the fruit of the *Spirit*, then there is no doubt. Here are the fruit of the Spirit listed in Galatians 5:22,23: love, joy, peace, long-suffering, gentleness, goodness, faith, meekness, and temperance.

> "If we live in the *Spirit,* let us also walk in the *Spirit.*"
>
> Galatians 5:25

The Will of God Part Three

Paul's benediction to the Galatians is:

> "Brethren, the *grace* of our Lord Jesus Christ be with your spirit. Amen."
> Galatians 6:18

Paul greets the saints in Ephesus:

> "*Grace* be to you, and peace, from God our Father, and from the Lord Jesus Christ."
> Ephesians 1:2

We should be *holy* and without blame before Him in love. We have been *adopted* as children of God by Jesus Christ to himself, according to the good pleasure of His *Will* (or by the wonderful *Will of God*), to the praise of His glorious *grace*, wherein He has made us acceptable in the Beloved (Jesus is the beloved Son of God, and/or God the Son), in whom we have salvation through His blood, the forgiveness of sins, according to the riches of His *grace* (Ephesians 1:4-6).

> "After that ye heard the word of *truth*, the gospel of your salvation: in whom also, after that ye believed, ye were sealed with that *Holy Spirit* of promise, Which is the earnest [pledge] of our inheritance."
> Ephesians 1:13,14

> "For by *grace* are ye saved through faith; and that not of yourselves; it is the gift of God."
> Ephesians 2:8

I feel *grace* means holiness, without which no man shall see God. Verses 11 and 12 tell us that since we are Gentiles (if we are), we are not included in the *Old Will of God*. We were aliens and strangers from the *Will*, having no hope and without God in the world.

But now we *all*, both Jew and Gentile, have access to the Father God by one *Spirit* (Ephesians 2:18).

> "Now therefore ye are no more strangers and foreigners, but fellow citizens with the saints, and of the household of God; And are built upon the foundation of the apostles and prophets, Jesus Christ himself being the chief cornerstone; In whom all the building fitly framed together groweth unto a *holy* temple in the Lord: In whom ye also are builded together for a habitation [dwelling place] of God through the *Spirit*."
> Ephesians 2:19-22

"If ye have heard of the dispensation [a system of revealed commands and promises regulating human affairs] of the *grace* of God which is given to me [Paul] to you-ward . . . " (Ephesians 3:2). Paul tells us in verses 3-6 that God revealed this to him by revelation and now it is no longer a mystery. In other ages it was not made known to the sons of men, but is now revealed to the *holy* apostles and prophets by the *Spirit*. Now the Gentiles are fellow heirs, and of the same body, and partakers of His promise in Christ by the gospel.

> "Whereof I [Paul] was made a minister, according to the gift of the *grace* of God given unto me by the effectual working of his *power*."
> Ephesians 3:7

The main points I would like for you to see in Ephesians 3 are: "To be *strengthened* with *might* by his *Spirit* in the

The Will of God Part Three

inner man" (verse 16) and "That ye might be filled with all the fullness of God" (verse 19).

"Now unto him that is able to do exceeding abundantly above all that we ask or think, according to the *power* that worketh in *us*."
Ephesians 3:20

"But unto everyone of us is given *grace* according to the measure of the gift of Christ."
Ephesians 4:7

"Be renewed [made new] in the spirit of your mind . . . Put on the new man, which after God is created in righteousness and *true holiness* . . . Putting away lying [bearing false witness against your neighbor] . . . Be ye angry, and sin not . . . Neither give place to the devil [do not give the devil a foothold]."
Ephesians 4:23-27

"Let no corrupt communication proceed out of your mouth, but that which is good to the use of edifying, that it may minister *grace* unto the hearer, And grieve not the *Holy Spirit* of God, whereby ye are sealed unto the day of redemption [salvation]."
Ephesians 4:29,30

"Be ye not unwise, but understanding what the *will of the Lord* is . . . Be filled with the *Spirit* . . . Making melody in your heart to the Lord; Giving thanks always for all things unto God and the Father in the name of our Lord Jesus Christ."
Ephesians 5:17-20

God's Will

"Be strong in the Lord, and in the *power* of his might. Put on the whole armor of God [the entire Will of God]."

Ephesians 6:10,11

"For we wrestle not against flesh and blood, but against principalities, against powers, against the rulers of the darkness of this world, against spiritual wickedness in high places."

Ephesians 6:12

"Take unto you the whole armor of God, that ye may be able to withstand in the evil day, and having done all to stand" (Ephesians 6:13). Yes, power to stand when evil is present. "Girt about with *truth* [the Holy Spirit], and having on the breastplate of righteousness; and your feet shod with the . . . gospel of peace [Jesus Christ is the Prince of Peace]" (Ephesians 6:14,15).

"Above all, taking the shield of faith [gift of the Holy Spirit], wherewith ye shall be able to quench all the fiery darts of the wicked. And take the helmet of salvation, and the sword of the *Spirit*, which is the word of God."

Ephesians 6:16,17

"*Grace* be with all them that love our Lord Jesus Christ in sincerity. Amen."

Ephesians 6:24

"For our gospel came not unto you in word only, but also in *power,* and in the *Holy Ghost.*"

1 Thessalonians 1:5

"Ye became followers of us, and of the Lord, hav-

ing received the word in much affliction, with joy of the *Holy Ghost*."
1 Thessalonians 1:6

"For this is the will of God, even your sanctification, that ye should abstain from fornication: That every one of you should know how to possess his vessel in sanctification and honor . . . For God hath not called us unto uncleanness, but unto holiness. He therefore that despiseth, despiseth not man, but God, who hath also given unto us his Holy Spirit."
1 Thessalonians 4:3,4,7,8

You are taught of God to love one another (verse 9). Remember that love is the fulfillment of the commandments.

"The very God of peace [Jesus Christ] *sanctify* you wholly; and I pray God your whole spirit, and soul and body be preserved blameless unto the coming of our Lord Jesus Christ. Faithful is he that calleth you, who also will do it."
1 Thessalonians 5:23,24

Do what? Sanctify you, that's what!

"But we are bound to give thanks always to God for you, brethren beloved of the Lord, because God hath from the beginning chosen you to salvation through sanctification of the Spirit and belief of the truth."
2 Thessalonians 2:13

"But the Lord is faithful, who shall stablish you,

and keep you from evil."
2 Thessalonians 3:3

"Let every one that nameth the name of Christ depart from iniquity."
2 Timothy 2:19

"If a man therefore purge himself from these, he shall be a vessel unto honor, *sanctified*, and meet [useful] for the master's use, and prepared unto every good work. Flee youthful lusts [passions]: but follow righteousness, faith, charity [love], peace, with them that call on the Lord out of a *pure heart*."
2 Timothy 2:21,22

"Not by works of righteousness which we have done, but according to his mercy he saved us, by the washing of regeneration, and renewing of the *Holy Ghost*. Which he shed on us abundantly through Christ Jesus our Savior; That being justified by his *grace*, we should be made *heirs* according to the hope of eternal life."
Titus 3:5-7

"How shall we escape, if we neglect so great salvation; which at the first began to be spoken by the Lord, and was confirmed unto us by them that heard him; God also bearing them witness, both with signs and wonders, and with divers [various] miracles, and gifts of the *Holy Ghost*, according to his own *will*? For both he that *sanctifieth*, and they who are *sanctified are all of one* [when we are sanctified, we are one with Jesus, God the Father, and the Holy Spirit]: for which cause he is not

The Will of God Part Three

ashamed to call them brethren."
Hebrews 2:3,4,11

"Therefore leaving the principles of the doctrine of Christ, let us go on unto perfection; not laying again the foundation of repentance from dead works, and of faith toward God . . . For it is impossible for those who were once enlightened, and have tasted of the heavenly gift, and were made partakers of the Holy Ghost, And have tasted the good word of God, and the powers of the world to come, If they shall fall away, to renew them again unto repentance; seeing they crucify to themselves the Son of God afresh, and put him to an open shame. But that which beareth thorns and briers is rejected, and is nigh unto cursing; whose end is to be burned. But, beloved, we are persuaded better things of you."
Hebrews 6:1,4-6,8,9

"Follow peace with all men, and *holiness*, without which no man shall see the Lord."
Hebrews 12:14

"Now the God of peace, that brought again from the dead our Lord Jesus, that great shepherd of the sheep, through the blood of the everlasting *covenant* [*testament*], Make you perfect in every good work to do his *will*, working in you that which is well-pleasing in his sight, through Jesus Christ; to whom be glory for ever and ever. Amen."
Hebrews 13:20,21

"But as he which hath called you is *holy*, be ye *holy* in all manner of conversation; Because it is

God's Will

written, Be ye *holy;* for I am *holy*. Seeing ye have *purified* your souls in obeying the *truth* through the *Spirit* unto unfeigned love of the brethren, see that ye love one another with a *pure heart* fervently."
1 Peter 1:15,16,22

John tells what the truth is: "It is the *Spirit* that beareth witness, because the *Spirit* is *truth"* (1 John 5:6).

"For there are three that bear record in heaven, the Father, the Word [Jesus Christ], and the *Holy Ghost:* and these three are one. And there are three that bear witness in earth, the *Spirit*, and the water, and the blood: and these three agree in one."
1 John 5:7,8

The three are united in *love* for the good of mankind, because all three are love.

BLESSED

How are holy people supposed to live? Follow the word *blessed* in the Scriptures and you will know.

Matthew 5:3-12 connotes possessing strength and power. The word *blessed* is a very powerful word. I feel the word *blessed* means *holy*. If Jesus had said *holy* in place of *blessed,* more than likely no one would have understood. Many today do not understand. Remember that Jesus came to baptize with the *Holy Ghost* (see Matthew 3:11, Mark 1:8, Luke 3:16, John 1:33, Acts 1:5, Acts 11:16), and at this point in time the *Holy Ghost* had not come to all mankind. *Holiness* is here now and is for all mankind, if we will accept and do His Will.

"Follow peace with all men, and *holiness* [sanctification], without which no man shall see the Lord."

Hebrews 12:14

"*Blessed* [holy] are the poor in spirit: for theirs is the kingdom of heaven. *Blessed* [holy] are they which do hunger and thirst after righteousness: for they shall be filled. *Blessed* [holy] are the pure in heart: for they shall see God. *Blessed* [holy] are the peacemakers: for they shall be called the children of God. *Blessed* [holy] are they which are persecuted for righteousness' sake: for theirs is the kingdom of heaven. *Blessed* [holy] are ye, when men shall revile you, and persecute you, and shall say all manner of evil against you falsely, for my sake. Rejoice, and be exceeding glad: for great is your *reward in heaven*: for so persecuted they the prophets which were before you."

Matthew 5:3,6,8-12

God's Will

If you desire to be a peacemaker, seek holiness.

If you desire to be a child of God, seek holiness.

If you desire to inherit the kingdom of heaven, seek holiness.

If you desire to see God, seek holiness.

Blessed must mean *holy* or else the writer of Hebrews 12:14 is wrong. Remember this, without *holiness* no man shall see the Lord.

Let us consider Mary and Elisabeth before the birth of Jesus and John the Baptist. Mary was told by an angel sent from God that the child she would bear was *holy*, and called the Son of God (Luke 1:26-38). The angel also told Mary her cousin Elisabeth, who was well stricken in years, was with child. Elisabeth is the mother of John. Mary went to visit Elisabeth (verse 41). When she entered Elisabeth's home and spoke to her, Elisabeth was filled with the Holy Ghost and her baby (John) was also filled with the Holy Ghost. This was foretold to Zechariah (John's father) by an angel (Luke 1:15).

Elisabeth began to exercise the Holy Spirit's gift of discernment (Luke 1:42; 1 Corinthians 12:10). Speaking with a loud voice, Elisabeth said to Mary, *"Blessed* [Holy] art thou among women, and *blessed* [Holy] is the fruit of thy womb [Jesus]" (verse 42). There is no evidence that Elisabeth knew anything about the things that had happened to Mary, and yet she called Mary and the baby (Jesus) *blessed* (holy). This manifestation was truly a gift of the *Holy Spirit*. Then Elisabeth said to Mary, "Whence is this to me, that the mother of my Lord should come to me? For, lo, as soon as the voice of thy salutation sounded in mine ears, the babe leaped in my womb for joy" (verses 43,44). Elisabeth began to prophesy (another gift of the Holy Ghost):

> "And *blessed* [holy] is she that believed: for there shall be a performance of those things which were told her [Mary] from the Lord."
> Luke 1:45

The word *blessed* spoken by Elisabeth concerning Mary can only mean *holy*. The word *blessed* concerning the baby Jesus, can mean only one thing, *holy*.

The gifts of the *Holy Spirit* that Elisabeth made manifest speak of holiness. Mary also, began to manifest the gifts of the Spirit:

Mary began to exercise the Holy Spirit's gift of prophecy. "And Mary said, My soul doth magnify the Lord, and my spirit hath rejoiced in God my Savior" (Luke 1:47).

Mary is a living example of being humble:

> "For he hath regarded the low estate of his handmaiden."
> Luke 1:48

> "*Blessed* [holy] are the poor [humble] in spirit: for theirs is the kingdom of heaven."
> Matthew 5:3

Mary prophesied saying:

> "All generations shall call me *blessed* [holy; this has happened as she prophesied]. For he that is mighty hath done to me great things; and *holy* is his name. And his mercy is on them that fear him from generation to generation."
> Luke 1:48-50

Jesus said:

God's Will

"*Blessed* [holy] are the merciful: for they shall obtain mercy."

Matthew 5:7

Mary prophesied:
"He hath put down the mighty from their seats, and exalted them of low degree [the meek]."

Luke 1:52

Jesus said:
"*Blessed* [holy] are the meek: for they shall inherit the earth."

Matthew 5:5

Mary said:
"He hath filled the hungry with good things; and the rich he hath sent empty away."

Luke 1:53

Jesus said:
"*Blessed* [holy] are they which do hunger and thirst after righteousness [good things]: for they shall be filled."

Matthew 5:6

Mary was truly a *holy* woman in every scriptural way.

At one time I thought *blessed* meant *happy*, but I can't possibly think this any longer.

"*Blessed* [holy] are they that do his commandments, that they may have right to the tree of life, and may enter in through the gates into the city."

Revelation 22:14

It seems to me the Old Testament saints will someday

The Will of God Part Three

rise from their resting places and will have the opportunity to accept Jesus as Christ and will receive the gift of the *Holy Ghost* from the Father God through Jesus. They will then have the right to enter the city mentioned in Revelation 22:14, for without holiness (Hebrews 12:14) no man shall see God.

In chapter 2 we wrote about the New Covenant (Jeremiah 31:31-34). That covenant was given to the Old Testament saints, and they will receive it in God's time.

Have you received the Holy Spirit into your life? Remember this, Jesus came to baptize you with the Holy Ghost. All you have to do is ask Jesus (see Luke 11:9-13). Repent, believe, ask, receive. It is His *Will* to you.

God's Will

TRUE LOVE FROM THE TRINITY

The natural self is like a rope that is loose at both ends. It can't be pushed, but can be easily led or pulled. It tends to snap at others like a whip at the twinkling of an eye and has a natural tendency to hurt others either by the tongue or fist.

Love is like a ring. Love is never ending. Love is an active caring concern for others. Love does no harm to anyone or itself. Love tries to help others and always tries to bring others into its fellowship. Love goes about doing good to all people.

If there is any weak point in this ring of love, it will become evident in a short while. Weak love is evasive; it comes and goes and probably has a bad temper. It may explode into bad language and finds it very difficult to keep the ring together. The ring will break at this weak point. Weak love has a tendency to want to hurt others.

Can we say #2 is still love even though there is a weak spot in this love ring? We would have to say it has its weak point.

What is God? God is love, an endless eternal ring of love that will never change or die. God's love has no weak areas. No part of God's ring of love would tend to hurt anyone. This is the kind of love God really wants all mankind to have.

THE TRINITY

God the Father is Love. God the Son is Love. God the Holy Spirit is Love. There is no part of them that would hurt anyone in any way. All are God and all are Love. They all

The Will of God Part Three

agree . . . there is no animosity between them. They are united in Love, yet there is no bond, chain, or rope holding them together. Jesus prayed to His Father that *we* should be one with them, just as they are one.

In John 17:11, Jesus was praying. He asked the Father God to make His followers one, as they, God the Father and Jesus, are one. You may say to yourself, *I can't understand how God the Father, Jesus the Son, and the Holy Spirit are one, let alone me, becoming one with God.* The Trinity is Love. Love makes them one. Thus, one God.

Jesus asked God the Father that we also become Love. This means to me that we can be Love, and since we can, we can be one with God, just as Jesus prayed. We shall not be God, but will receive the strength and power that love brings. It is very important to know and do all the *Will of God*.

God the Father is in Heaven. Where is Jesus? Jesus is sitting at the right hand of the Father. Where is the Holy Spirit? The Holy Spirit is with mankind on earth. The three are completely separate, but still united by Love, and have a desire to be at peace with the others of the Trinity. The Trinity wants all mankind to be united by the same love. His desire is that man should place God (love) first, then, loving your neighbor as yourself will be no problem. Then even though we are not standing holding hands and singing hymns together, we can still love each other. We cannot love the way God planned unless we accept all of the *Will of God*. Why not accept His *Will*?

God's Will

Sounds great to me!

The wonderful Holy Spirit can remove that weak part of man that is rebellious against God and man. He will give us power to overcome that part of our lives that tends to hurt God and other people. This power is a gift from God through the Holy Spirit, and the Holy Spirit is part of the wonderful *Will of God*.

Why not let the *Holy Spirit* bring the ends of your life together, forming this endless ring of love in your life? It is accomplished by allowing God to be first place in your life. Then that weak point in your ring of love will be refurbished and strengthened, allowing you to be one with God the Father and Jesus Christ. "Present your bodies a living sacrifice, holy, acceptable unto God, which is your reasonable service, and be not conformed to this world: but be ye transformed by the renewing of your mind, that ye may prove what is that good, and acceptable, and perfect, *will of God*" (Romans 12:1,2).

Review Luke 11:9-13. If you don't have the strength I have been writing about, if you want to receive the Holy Spirit, just ask Jesus and He will give you these wonderful gifts which are part of the *Will of God.* If you have not received the *Holy Spirit* into your life, ask and you will receive.

Chapter 7

Summary

God knows your weakest point and so does Satan. God understands your temptations and sent the Holy Spirit into our world to give us spiritual strength. Yes, strength to overcome the evil one.

The Holy Spirit also brought gifts to mankind. They are part of God's wonderful Will.

The Holy Spirit is the third person of the Trinity. He is also called the Comforter.

Grace, blessed, sanctification, and *sanctify* all relate to holiness, or "to make holy."

If you desire to receive the Holy Spirit into your life, ask Jesus. He is part of God's Will to you. Talk to Jesus; He would like very much to hear from you. His Will is for you, if by faith, you will receive it.

CHAPTER 8

THE WILL OF GOD PART FOUR

The fourth part of My Will to you is eternal life with Us. Yes, life without end. Please believe Me when I say it is not My Will that any should perish. I am preparing a place for you that will be beyond your grandest imagination. Life eternal is My Will for you. At times it may seem that I am not close to you, but I am.

EVERLASTING LIFE—THE LIFE-ETERNAL LIFE ABUNDANT LIFE—REST FOR THE SOUL— THE RESURRECTION THE KINGDOM OF HEAVEN

By faith I have accepted all the wonderful gifts from God the Father through Jesus Christ and the Holy Spirit. I am so thankful to be called a son of God. This title was given to me by His Last *Will* and *Testament.* I am so happy to come into a more complete understanding of His gifts, and now by faith I am ready for eternal life, when my physical life on earth ends.

The words *everlasting life, the life-eternal life,* and *abundant life,* all relate to rest for the soul, the resurrection of the dead, and the kingdom of Heaven.

Let us begin to walk through the wonderful promises from God, and let them fill your present life with joy as they have for me.

"Blessed are the poor in spirit [humble]: for theirs is the *kingdom of heaven"* (Matthew 5:3). "Blessed are they which are persecuted for righteousness' sake: for theirs is the *kingdom of heaven"* (verse 10). "Blessed are ye, when men shall revile you, and persecute you, and say all manner of evil against you falsely, for my sake" (verse 11). "Rejoice, and be exceeding glad: for great is your reward in *heaven"* (verse 12).

> "Therefore I say unto you, Take no thought for your life, what ye shall eat, or what ye shall drink; nor yet for your body, what ye shall put on. Is not *the life* more than meat, and the body more than raiment? But seek ye first the *kingdom of God,* and his righteousness; and all these things shall be added unto you."
>
> Matthew 6:25,33

The Will of God Part Four

These are very familiar verses which speak of life—life now and eternal life. Jesus suggests to you that you place God first in this life and not worry about food or clothing. If you place the *kingdom of God* first, all the necessities of life will be added to you. Don't worry about tomorrow.

Now here is the big question. Can you accept these promises of *abundant life*? The choice is yours alone.

"Come unto me all ye that labor and are heavy laden, and I will give you rest. Take my yoke upon you, and learn of me; for I am meek and lowly in heart: and ye shall find *rest* unto your souls. For my yoke is easy, and my burden is light."
Matthew 11:28-30

Jesus speaks of the *kingdom of God* as a mystery in Matthew 13. "It is given unto you to know the mysteries of the *kingdom of heaven*" (verse 11). Some will understand the parables concerning the *kingdom of God* and some will not. Those who have understanding will receive "more abundance: but whosoever hath not, from him shall be taken away even that which he hath" (verse 12). Some will hear and not understand. Some will see and not perceive (verse 13). We all need to search the Scriptures so we will know and understand what the *Will of God* is.

"Good Master, what good thing shall I do, that I may have *eternal life*?" (Matthew 19:6). Jesus quoted some of the Ten Commandments verses 17-19) concerning love for your neighbor. Then the man said, "All these things have I kept from my youth up: what lack I yet?" (Matthew 19:20).

Notice that Jesus did not quote the commandments concerning how to love God above all else. I feel this man's problem was he could not place God first in his life. He was not willing to give up his riches and follow Christ. Giving away all his money to the poor really turned him off. Jesus

God's Will

(God) knew what his problem was before he asked the question. I don't think the man really understood the law of love, which is placing God first, for God is love. It seems to me he knew the law but didn't understand it, nor did he really love his neighbor as himself. Needless to say, the young man went away sorrowful, never to have eternal life, unless he was later converted.

> "And everyone that hath forsaken houses, or brethren, or sisters, or father, or mother, or wife, or children, or lands, for my name's sake, shall receive an hundredfold, and shall inherit *everlasting life.*"
>
> Matthew 19:29

Jesus is speaking at this point about the judgment of nations:

> "Then shall the King say unto them on his right hand, Come ye blessed [holy] of my Father, inherit the kingdom prepared for you from the foundation of the world. Then shall he say also unto them on the left hand, Depart from me, ye cursed, into everlasting fire, prepared for the devil and his angels. And these shall go away into everlasting punishment: but the righteous into *life eternal.*"
>
> Matthew 25:34,41,46

Make the right choice. Don't let your soul suffer the fire of everlasting punishment.

> "And Jesus answered and said, Verily I say unto you, There is no man that hath left house, or brethren, or sisters, or father, or mother, or wife, or children, or lands, for my sake, and the

The Will of God Part Four

gospel's. But he shall receive an hundredfold now in this time, houses, and brethren, and sisters, and mothers, and children, and lands, with persecutions; and in the world to come eternal life."
Mark 10:29,30

Total commitment will yield a hundredfold benefits in this time and in the world to come, *eternal life*. Did you notice the word *persecutions* in verse 30? It sticks out like a sore thumb. Even if your name is Paul, you will have problems in this world. Being a Christian does not make you immune to trouble. That's why God made us with a brain. You are not, nor will you ever be, a puppet on a string. God has given us a guide to life, love, and holiness through His Word and it's up to us to use this guide. You can know this for sure: God will not leave His own. At times it may seem that God is not close to you but He is. Search the Word: Psalm 37:23-29, Matthew 6:28-34.

"A man's life consisteth not in the abundance of things he possesseth" (Luke 12:15). Don't get greedy, for possessions do not make *life* abundant. Did that hurt a little bit? It did me, but go on—it is worth it.

Because he believed that Jesus did indeed have a kingdom, Jesus told the thief on the cross who was hanging there beside Him:

"Verily I say unto thee, today shalt thou be with me in *paradise*."
Luke 23:43

"In him [Jesus] was *life;* and the *life* was the light of men."
John 1:4

"That whosoever believeth in him should not

God's Will

perish, but have *eternal life*. For God so loved the world, that he gave his only begotten Son, that whosoever believeth in him should not perish, but have *everlasting life*. For God sent not his Son into the world to condemn the world; but that the world through him might be saved. He that believeth on the Son [Jesus] hath *everlasting life*: and he that believeth not the Son shall not see *life*; but the wrath of God abideth on him."

John 3:15-17,36

"But whosoever drinketh of the water that I [Jesus] shall give him shall never thirst; but the water that I shall give him shall be in him a well of water springing up into *everlasting life*."

John 4:14

"Jesus saith unto them, My meat is to do the *will* of him that sent me, and to finish his work."

John 4:34

In verse 36 He speaks again of *eternal life*. Teach others about the *Will of God* and win others, and both he that teaches and he that receives will rejoice together in *eternal life*. Jesus said:

"Verily, verily, I say unto you, He that heareth my word, and believeth on him that sent me, hath *everlasting life*, and shall not come into condemnation but is passed from death unto life."

John 5:24

"The dead shall hear the voice of the Son of God: and they that hear shall *live*."

John 5:26

The Will of God Part Four

Jesus said:

> "Search the scriptures; for in them ye think ye have *eternal life*: and they are they [the Scriptures] which testify of me. And ye will not come to me, that ye might have *life* . . . But I know you, that ye have *not* the love of God in you."
>
> John 5:39,40,42

Do not be deceived. Know the *will* of God and do it.

> "Labor not for the meat which perisheth, but for that meat which endureth unto *everlasting life*, which the Son of man [Jesus] shall give unto you: for him hath God the Father sealed."
>
> John 6:27

> "And this is the Father's *will* which hath sent me, that of all which he hath given me I should lose nothing, but should raise it up again at the last day. And this is the *will* of him that sent me, that everyone which seeth the Son [Jesus], and believeth on him, may have *everlasting life*: and I will raise him up at the last day."
>
> John 6:39,40

> "Verily, verily, I say unto you, He that believeth on me [Jesus] hath *everlasting life*."
>
> John 6:47

> "It is the Spirit that quickeneth [makes alive]; the flesh profiteth [helps] nothing: the words that I speak unto you, they are spirit, and they are *life*. But there are some of you that believe not."
>
> John 6:63,64

God's Will

"Simon Peter answered him [Jesus], Lord, to whom shall we go? thou hast the words of *eternal life*."
John 6:68

Jesus is the only one who can give *eternal life*.

"The thief cometh not, but for to steal, and to kill, and to destroy: I [Jesus] am come that they might have *life*, and that they might have it more abundantly. I am the good shepherd: the good shepherd giveth his *life* for the sheep."
John 10:10,11

"And other sheep I have, which are not of this fold [other nations, other tribes, all who will accept His Will; men, women, children, whether they be bond or free, rich or poor]: them also must I bring, and they shall hear my voice; and there shall be one fold, and one shepherd."
John 10:16

"My sheep hear my voice, and I know them, and they follow me: And I give unto them eternal life; and they shall never perish, neither shall any man pluck them out of my hand. My Father, which gave them me, is greater than all; and no man is able to pluck them out of my Father's hand. I [Jesus] and my Father are one."
John 10:27-30

The Father and the Son and the Holy Spirit are one. They are all love, all united for the good of man. They are doing everything they can to get you and me to see the tremendous possibilities and opportunities afforded through this wonderful *Will of God*.

The Will of God Part Four

"He that loveth his life shall lose it; and he that hateth his life in this world shall keep it unto *life eternal*. If any man serve me [Jesus], let him follow me; and *where I am*, there shall also my servant be: if any man serve me, him will my Father honor."
John 12:25,26

"I [Jesus] know that his [the Father's] commandment is *life everlasting*: whatsoever I speak therefore, even as the Father said unto me, so I speak."
John 12:50

In John 17 Jesus is praying to His Father for His own that He should give *eternal life* to as many as God the Father has given Him.

"These words spake Jesus, and lifted up his eyes to heaven, and said, Father, the hour is come; glorify thy Son, that thy Son also may glorify thee: As thou hast given him power over all flesh, that he should give eternal life to as many as thou hast given him. And this is life eternal, that they might know thee the only true God, and Jesus Christ, whom thou hast sent."
John 17:1-3

"Holy Father, keep through thine own name those whom thou hast given me, that they be one, as we are. While I was with them in the world, I kept them in thy name: those that thou gavest me I have kept, and none of them is lost, but the son of perdition [Judas Iscariot]; that the scripture might be fulfilled."
John 17:11,12

God's Will

"I pray . . . that thou shouldest keep them from the evil. They are not of the world, even as I am not of the world."
John 17:15

"Father, I *will* that they also, whom thou hast given me, be with me where I am, that they may behold my glory, which thou hast given me: for thou lovedst me before the foundation of the world. And I have declared unto them thy name, and will declare it: that the love wherewith thou hast loved me may be in them, and I in them."
John 17:24,26

Acts 3:15 says Jesus is the Prince of *Life*.

"Then Paul and Barnabas [speaking to the Jews] waxed bold, and said, It was necessary that the word of God should first have been spoken to you: but seeing ye put it from you, and judge yourselves unworthy of *everlasting life*, lo, we turn to the Gentiles. And when the Gentiles heard this, they were glad, and glorified the word of the Lord: and as many as were ordained to *eternal life* believed."
Acts 13:46,48

Romans 2:6 tells us God will render to every man according to his deeds.

"To them who by patient continuance in well-doing seek for glory and honor and *immortality*, *eternal life*: But unto them that are contentious, and do not obey the truth, but obey unrighteousness, indignation and wrath, Tribulation and

The Will of God Part Four

anguish, upon every soul of man that doeth evil, of the Jew first, and also of the Gentile; But glory, honor, and peace, to every man that worketh good; to the Jew first, and also to the Gentile. For there is no respect of persons with God."
Romans 2:7-11

Romans 6:4 says we also should walk in newness of *life*. We shall also *live* with Him, dead unto sin, but *alive* unto God through Jesus Christ.

"But now being made free from sin, and become servants to God, ye have your fruit unto holiness, and the end *everlasting life*. For the wages of sin is death; but the gift of God is *eternal life* through Jesus Christ our Lord."
Romans 6:22,23

"For to be carnally minded is death: but to be spiritually minded is *life* and peace."
Romans 8:6

"Who [God] also hath made us able ministers of the *new testament*; not of the letter, but of the spirit: for the letter killeth, but the spirit giveth *life*."
2 Corinthians 3:6

"The things which are seen are temporal; but the things which are not seen are *eternal*."
2 Corinthians 4:18

"For he that soweth to his flesh shall of the flesh reap corruption [death]; but he that soweth to the Spirit shall of the Spirit reap *life everlasting*."
Galatians 6:8

God's Will

"When Christ, who is our *life*, shall appear, then shall ye also appear with him in glory."
Colossians 3:4

"But thou, O man of God, flee these things [mentioned in verses 1-10]; and follow after righteousness, godliness, faith, love, patience, meekness. Fight the good fight of faith, lay hold on eternal life, whereunto thou art also called, and hast professed a good profession before many witnesses."
1 Timothy 6:11,12

"Charge them that are rich in this world, that they be not high-minded, nor trust in uncertain riches, but in the living God, who giveth us richly all things to enjoy; That they do good, that they be rich in good works, ready to distribute, willing to communicate; Laying up in store for themselves a good foundation against the time to come, that they may lay hold on *eternal life*."
1 Timothy 6:17-19

"Therefore I endure all things for the elect's sakes, that they may also obtain the salvation which is in Christ Jesus with eternal glory. It is a faithful saying: For if we be dead with him, we shall also live with him: If we suffer, we shall also reign with him: if we deny him, he also will deny us."
2 Timothy 2:10-12

"In hope of *eternal life*, which God, that cannot lie, promised before the world began."
Titus 1:2

"That being justified by his grace, we should be

The Will of God Part Four

made heirs according to the hope of *eternal life*."
Titus 3:7

"And being made perfect, he [Jesus] became the author of *eternal salvation* unto all them that obey him."
Hebrews 5:9

"Neither by the blood of goats and calves, but by his own blood he entered in once into the holy place, having obtained *eternal redemption* for us."
Hebrews 9:12

Hebrews 9:15 refers to "the promise of *eternal inheritance*." Remember that Jesus brought to mankind the wonderful *Will of God*, through which we can receive this eternal inheritance.

"Blessed is the man that endureth temptation: for when he is tried, he shall receive the crown of *life*, which the Lord hath promised to them that love him."
James 1:12

If we resist temptation, we shall receive the crown of *life*. Temptation in itself is not sin, it becomes sin when the thought becomes a plan of action.

"Then when lust hath conceived, it bringeth forth sin: and sin, when it is finished, bringeth forth death."
James 1:15

Look at the words *conceived* and *conceive*. I feel the

God's Will

words mean the same, to become pregnant, as the word is used in Matthew 1:18-22. "Joseph, thou son of David, fear not to take unto thee Mary thy wife: for that which is conceived in her is of the Holy Ghost" (Matthew 18:20). The two words, *conceived* and *conceive,* are mentioned in the Old and New Testaments fifty-nine times, and only five times do they mean "a thought." Even the five times connote the afore mentioned meaning.

When a woman conceives there is one thing for sure, she will bring a child into this world. By the same token we can say that when lust has conceived, it has no recourse but to bring forth sin. I feel that this will help to explain Matthew 5:27,28 when Jesus taught on the subject of adultery. He says in verse 27, "Thou shalt not commit adultery."

> "But I say unto you, That whosoever looketh on a woman to lust after her hath committed adultery with her already in his heart [mind]."
>
> Matthew 5:28

The mind has conceived the thought: therefore, adultery will take place because the mind is "made up" or determined to do it. Consequently, sin has taken place in the mind, even before the act. In other words, when a plan of action has taken place in the mind that is the moment when sin has taken place, because you are determined to commit the act of adultery. If we expect to receive the crown of *life*, we must resist temptation.

> "And this is the promise that he hath promised us, even *eternal life.*"
>
> 1 John 2:25

> "And this is the record, that God hath given to us *eternal life*, and this *life* is in his Son [Jesus]. He

that hath the Son hath *life*; and he that hath not the Son of God hath not *life*. These things have I written unto you that believe on the name of the Son of God; that ye may know that ye have *eternal life*, and that ye may believe on the name of the Son of God."
1 John 5:11-13

"Keep yourselves in the love of God, looking for the mercy of our Lord Jesus Christ unto *eternal life*."
Jude 1:21

"To him that overcometh, will I [Jesus] give to eat of the tree of *life*, which is in the midst of the paradise of God . . . Be faithful unto death, and I will give thee a crown of *life* . . . He that overcometh shall not be hurt of the second death . . . To him that overcometh will I give to eat of the hidden manna, and will give him a white stone, and in the stone a new name written, which no man knoweth saving he that receiveth it . . . And he that overcometh, and keepeth my works unto the end, to him will I give power over the nations."
Revelation 2:7,10,11,17,26

"He that overcometh, the same shall be clothed in white raiment; and I will not blot out his name out of the book of *life*, but I will confess his name before my Father, and before his angels . . . Him that overcometh will I make a pillar in the temple of my God, and he shall go no more out: I will write upon him the name of my God, and the name of the city of my God, which is the new Jerusalem, which cometh down out of heaven

God's Will

from my God: and I will write upon him my new name . . . To him that overcometh will I grant to sit with me in my throne, even as I also overcame, and am set down with my Father in his throne."
Revelation 3:5,12,21

THE RESURRECTION

> "But as touching the *resurrection* of the dead, have ye not read that which was spoken unto you by God, saying, I am the God of Abraham, and the God of Isaac, and the God of Jacob? God is not the God of the dead, but of the *living*."
> Matthew 22:31,32

After Jesus was *resurrected*, others were *resurrected* at the same time and were seen by many people (Matthew 27:52). One day, maybe soon, all the saints who know and do the *Will of God* will *rise* to meet Jesus Christ in the air. There, we will be made perfect and will dwell with Him *eternally*.

Do good to those who find it difficult, if not impossible, to repay you and you will receive your reward at the *resurrection* of the just (Luke 14:13,14).

> "Marvel not at this: for the hour is coming, in the which all that are in the graves shall hear his voice, And shall come forth; they that have done good, unto the *resurrection of life*; and they that have done evil, unto the *resurrection* of damnation."
> John 5:28,29

Jesus told Martha that her brother Lazarus would *rise again*. Martha replied, "I know that he shall rise again in the *resurrection* at the last day. Jesus said unto her, I am the *resurrection*, and the *life*: he that believeth in me, though he were dead, yet shall he *live*: And whosoever liveth and believeth in me *shall never die*. Believest thou this?" (John 11:25,26).

In John 11:43,44, Jesus called Lazarus from the grave bound hand and foot with grave clothes and his face bound

God's Will

about with a napkin. Lazarus had been dead for four days. Jesus said, "Loose him, and let him go." Can you imagine the rejoicing of his friends and loved ones? Can you further imagine the rejoicing on the *Resurrection* Day when all the saints will *rise* from their graves? Can you imagine the rejoicing when we see our Lord Jesus who has brought this wonderful time to pass?

Pause for a moment. Let your mind dwell on this *Resurrection* Day, and give thanks and praise to the Father, Son, and Holy Spirit for this wonderful *Will of God*.

> "For if we have been planted together in the likeness of his death, we shall be also in the likeness of his *resurrection*: Knowing this, that our old man is crucified with him, that the body of sin might be destroyed, that henceforth we should not serve sin. For he that is dead is freed from sin. Now if we be dead with Christ, we believe that we shall also *live* with him: Knowing that Christ being raised from the dead dieth no more; death hath no more dominion over him. For in that he died, he died unto sin once: but in that he *liveth*, he *liveth* unto God."
>
> Romans 6:5-10

> "But if there be no *resurrection* of the dead, then is Christ not *risen*: And if Christ be not *risen*, then is our preaching vain, and your faith is also vain."
>
> 1 Corinthians 15:13,14

> "And if Christ be not raised, your faith is vain; ye are yet in your sins. Then they also which are fallen asleep in Christ are perished."
>
> 1 Corinthians 15:17,18

The Will of God Part Four

"But now is Christ *risen* from the dead, and become the firstfruits of them that slept. For since by man came death, by man came also the *resurrection* of the dead. For as in Adam all die, even so in Christ shall all be made *alive*. But every man in his own order: Christ the firstfruits; afterward they that are Christ's at his coming. Then cometh the end, when he shall have delivered up the kingdom to God."
1 Corinthians 15:20-24

"Behold, I show you a mystery; We shall not all sleep [be dead], but we shall all be changed, In a moment, in the twinkling of an eye, at the last trump: for the trumpet shall sound, and the dead shall be *raised* incorruptible [shall never decay], and we shall be changed. For this corruptible [body that will decay] must put on incorruption, and this mortal [sure to die sometime] must put on immortality [live on eternally] . . . Death is swallowed up in victory. O death, where is thy sting? O grave, where is thy victory? . . . But thanks be to God, which giveth us the victory through our Lord Jesus Christ."
1 Corinthians 15:51-57

Paul made the statement in Philippians 3:8-10 that all things of this earth is but so much refuse. The most important thing in this life is to have knowledge of Jesus Christ and the power of His *Resurrection*. In verse 14 Paul explains that he is pressing on toward the prize of the high calling of God in Christ Jesus. That prize is the *Resurrection unto life eternal*. That same prize is for all who know and do the complete *Will of God*. Let us strive to be perfect (mature) minded: and if any of us be less than perfect minded, "God

God's Will

shall reveal even this unto you" (verse 15).

If you want to be in the *Resurrection*, read God's Word, study to be like Christ, love God with all your heart (let Him be the very center of your life), with all your soul, with all your mind, and love your neighbor as yourself. This can be accomplished by knowing and doing all the *Will of God*.

In 2 Timothy 2:16-18 Paul says: "Shun profane and vain babblings" for there will be those who will teach that the *Resurrection* is already past, but pay no attention to such teaching, for they have erred. "The Lord knoweth them that are his. And, let everyone that nameth the name of Christ depart from iniquity [evil wicked ways]" (verse 19). Purge yourselves from the things of this world such as silver and gold, and be a vessel unto honor, sanctified and ready for the Master's use, and prepared unto every good work (verses 20,21).

> "Blessed be the God and Father of our Lord Jesus Christ, which according to his abundant mercy hath begotten [born] us again unto a *lively* [living] hope by the *resurrection* of Jesus Christ from the dead, To an inheritance incorruptible [which cannot decay], and undefiled, and that fadeth not away, reserved in *heaven* for you, Who are kept by the power of God through faith unto salvation ready to be revealed in the last time."
>
> 1 Peter 1:3-5

> "Behold, I come quickly; and my reward is with me, to give to every man according as his work shall be. I [Jesus] am Alpha and Omega, the beginning and the end, the first and the last. Blessed are they that do his commandments, that they may have right to the *tree of life*, and may

enter in through the gates into *the city.*"
                                                Revelation 22:12-14

The words *Everlasting Life, The Life-Eternal Life, Abundant Life, Rest for the Soul, The Resurrection of Life,* and the *Kingdom of Heaven* probably mean more to you now than ever before. As for me, *life* more abundant began when I found and accepted the total *Will of God.*

Truly, it is a wonderful privilege to belong to the family of God. If you have accepted *God's Will* and are willing to do His *Will,* then you too are one with God, just as the Father, Son, and Holy Spirit are one. Now you too have this wonderful inheritance and are united in love for the good of mankind. You are now a son or daughter of God through this *Will,* and joint heirs with Jesus, who is Creator of the heavens and earth.

Let us all praise God the Father, God the Son, and give thanks to God the Holy Spirit for all they have done for mankind. Praise the Lord for the wonderful *Will of God.*

Chapter 8

Summary

Eternal life with God the Father, God the Son, and God the Holy Spirit. Do you want it?

Everlasting Life, The Life-Eternal Life, Abundant Life, The Resurrection, and The Kingdom of Heaven all relate to Rest for the Soul, and this is your eternal reward if you know and do the Will of God.

I shall eternally give praise to God the Father and God the Son and thanks to God the Holy Spirit for all they have done for mankind. No greater love could we know than the unending, never-dying love of God.

Dear friend, this is God's Will for you. All you need to do is accept it.

BIBLIOGRAPHY

[1] The World Book Dictionary
Doubleday and Company, Inc., 1969

[2] Webster's Seventh New Collegiate Dictionary
G and C Merriam Company, 1965 ed.

[3] King James Version of the Bible
Thomas Nelson Inc. Publishers, 1975

[4] The Holy Bible, New International Version
New York International Bible Society, 1978

Printed in the United States
R2400003B/R24PG8557D001BA-2